2)¡ ⟨ 3

I turned on the hot tub and, when it was warm, slid in. Was it watching Hayley strip off her clothes which had put me in the mood? These days I was monogamous with the water jet that bubbled furiously from the back of the seat on the right side. By sitting just so, I could get the jet stream to rush across my labia and hit right at my clitoris . . . The jet stream pulsated against me and I squirmed on the seat to get the fullest effect. My fingers went to my nipples and I turned off the world . . .

"Hi."

My eyes shot open and I swung in the water to face the voice. Hayley posed in a halo of moonlight, her naked, slim body black against the clouds.

"Were you watching me?"

"I plead guilty. Kitt may have planted trees so the neighbors can't see the pool, but I've got a clear shot at the hot tub from my window. I have to say, I enjoyed it almost as much as you did." She stepped into the water . . .

This book is a work of fiction, and where real people and places are mentioned by name, they are used in a fictitious way.

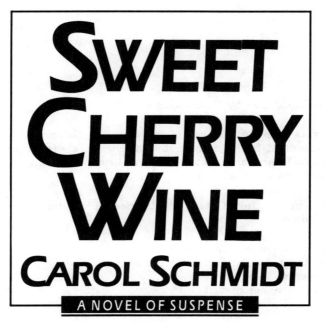

SWEET CHERRY WINE

CAROL SCHMIDT

A NOVEL OF SUSPENSE

The Naiad Press, Inc.
1994

Printed in the United States of America on acid-free paper
First Edition

Edited by Christine Cassidy
Cover design by Pat Tong and Bonnie Liss
    (Phoenix Graphics)
Typeset by Sandi Stancil

Library of Congress Cataloging-in-Publication Data

Schmidt, Carol, 1942–
    Sweet cherry wine / by Carol Schmidt.
        p.   cm.
    ISBN 1-56280-063-9
    1. Bars (Drinking establishments)—California—Los
Angeles—Fiction.   2. Women detectives—California—Los
Angeles—Fiction.   3. Lesbians—California—Los
Angeles—Fiction.   4. Los Angeles (Calif.)—Fiction.   I. Title.
PS3569.C51544S93   1994
813'.54—dc20   93-47345
                                                                              CIP

*This book is dedicated
to my 83-year-old father,
Emmett R. Schmidt,
a voracious reader
who always wanted me
to write mystery novels —
though Laney Samms
isn't quite the hero
he had in mind.*

About the Author

Carol Schmidt has been a newspaper reporter, publishing house editor, public relations director for a medical research institute affiliated with UCLA, and co-owner with Norma Hair of Words & Numbers, a business services firm in the Silverlake region of Los Angeles. Now, she and Norma live in a hundred-year-old church and school that they are turning into a home in rural Michigan, close to where they both grew up.

Her community involvement has included registering voters in the South in the '60s, organizing feminist consciousness-raising groups from 1968 through to the '80s, serving on the state board of California NOW, co-founding White Women Against Racism, and serving as co-chair of Sunset Junction Neighborhood Alliance, the organization which puts on the annual Sunset Junction Street Fair that brings together a quarter-million residents of Silverlake-Echo Park to celebrate their diversity.

Schmidt wrote reviews and a column ("Country Womyn/City Dyke") for the Los Angeles *Lesbian News* in the '80s and won three first-place writing awards from the National Gay and Lesbian Press Association. She has also been published in hundreds of newspapers, small magazines and anthologies. Author of *Silverlake Heat,* which also features Laney Samms, Schmidt is working on her third novel of suspense, to be published by Naiad in 1995.

PROLOGUE
June, 1960

"Bless me, Father, for I have sinned. This is my First Confession. I ate meat on Friday about a hundred times. I was angry at my parents and disobeyed them about a thousand times. I had impure thoughts and actions about a thousand times. I was jealous about a thousand times. I missed Mass about a hundred times. I used the Lord's name in vain about a hundred times. And I am guilty of one

1

murder. I am heartily sorry for these and all the sins of my past life, especially the murder."

Hayley gasped a deep breath and steeled herself for the priest to come rushing out of his cubicle and through the musty velvet drapes to grab her and take her to the police. What was taking him so long? Had he heard her? Couldn't he understand?

Grit dug into her kneecaps from the wooden kneeler. Lingering odors of garlic, sauerkraut, damp cement and melting wax made her nauseated. She thought once again of getting up and running for her life, before Father Sullivan could take in what she had just said, but her body wouldn't move. Better to stay, to have this whole thing over with, finally.

What would jail be like, she wondered over and over again.

Father Sullivan made a sound like a croaking bullfrog before he formed his first words. "That's an awful lot of sins for a little girl. Are you sure you did all those things?"

Of course she was sure — why would anybody make up sins? "Yes, Father. Umm, I'm not sure of the thousand timeses. Sister said we could guess the number."

"Yes. Well, um, how old are you, my child?"

"Ten."

"Did I hear you say something about a murder . . ."

This was it. Hayley's legs twitched and her left knee involuntarily jerked off of the kneeler and onto the concrete. She was sure the thumping sound would make Father Sullivan jump up and rush in to grab her before she could escape. Well, let him, then this whole thing would be over once and for all. Maybe her mom would come see her in prison.

"Are you all right, my child?"

"Yes, Father."

"You said you were angry a lot. Maybe you were angry at someone and then they died, and you think you might have caused it?"

"No, Father." She knew what she had done.

"Maybe you accidentally killed a pet, stepped on your turtle or something?"

What? Stepped on a turtle? He didn't believe her! What an idiot! Stupid priest, he was just as stupid as everybody else. Priests aren't special, or smart, they're stupid, stupid, stupid. She wouldn't have minded being taken off to jail by someone smart, but not by this nincompoop.

She got up off her knees and plunged through the dusty velvet, galloped out of the concrete cavern, yanked at the massive walnut doors and ran into the sunlight. She ran and ran till she was breathless, but she kept on running anyway, flying over the cracked sidewalk squares, fighting off a cramp under her left ribs. She leaped up the peeling gray-painted wooden front steps two at a time and disappeared into her bedroom, slamming the door shut so that her mother would stay out, at least long enough so that she could catch her breath and think.

So now she would have to keep on lying. She'd have to put on that dumb white dress for her mother tomorrow and take the communion wafer and swallow it without being cleansed of sin. She would *just have to put it out of her mind and pretend nothing had happened. She screwed up her eyes and tried to forget.*

Tears hovered but wouldn't fall. She set her teeth and waited for her mother to come in so she could lie some more.

CHAPTER ONE

"Hey, somebody's moving into that vacant building where you always park in the owner's space," I told Kitt.

"Damn!" Kitt looked up from her desk. She was taking forever to collect her notebook computer and all its gizmos so we could go home. It was late afternoon on a typical L.A. overcast June day, and Kitt's employees at Meyers Music Enterprises had long since left. Through peach miniblinds I was keeping watch on Kitt's new red Dodge Viper. I'd parked it in the alley across the street and around the corner from Santa Monica Boulevard.

I wondered again about the worth of owning an expensive sports car that you had to keep under guard. But then it sure had been fun driving it all day. Kitt loaned it to me because my old Chevy S-10 was in the garage again.

Five men in chino jumpsuits unloaded a moving van. Like a chorus line, bending and dipping and hoisting and marching, macho muscles rippling in rhythm, they transported hundreds of closed cardboard boxes into the mostly boarded-up building. From this vantage point I couldn't see anything through the few intact and unboarded window panes.

The oldest and stockiest of the men did the least work; his primary job seemed to be to keep checking the street both ways, as if he were waiting for someone. A loose chino jacket hung over his uniform.

"Who is it? What kind of business?" Kitt asked, pawing through a file drawer. Her tousled short dark hair fell in her eyes and she brushed it back roughly — not the way I'd treat the hundred-dollar haircut she'd gotten earlier that week. I'd had the same short wavy hairstyle back from my face since my twenties, when my dark hair had suddenly started to come in thick and silver and unmanageable any other way.

"Can't tell. Everything's unmarked. Nothing on the truck either."

"Huh. Probably a drug lab." Kitt grinned her crooked smile that, coupled with a few white streaks in her shag cut, deep dimples, and glistening black eyes, always reminded me of an English sheepdog. She put her load down on her teak desk and joined me at the window.

"Don't joke about things like that. You're probably right," I kidded back.

I glanced at an indentation in the wall in the alley, which apparently hid a door from view and from the elements. Something had moved in the back-set entrance, probably a dog. No, it was legs. Four legs. Two people were doing something on the ground. Probably having sex. I started to turn away when I realized that the naked legs, thinner, more like a woman's, were kicking and thrashing as if she were trying to get away.

"Kitt, look over there." I pointed.

Kitt slid open the window but we couldn't hear any noise.

"See that? He has his hand over her mouth — call nine-one-one," I said. "I'm going to help her."

I raced down the back stairs and into the alley behind Santa Monica Boulevard and across the side street. The movers glanced at me and at the man in front, the one who seemed to be waiting for some-one, all of them hesitating, their packages slowing in midair.

The stocky front-man scowled at me, his dark stare piercing me, and his hand went inside his jacket. He had one heavy black eyebrow running straight across his face like a shelf. His dark eyes shone out from under the ledge like an angry bear emerging from a cave.

"Stop!" he ordered.

I started to say "Fuck you" when I saw a flash

7

of metal. The hand inside the jacket brought out a gun. A big sucker, some kind of semiautomatic, an Uzi maybe. I stopped.

"What are you doing here?" he demanded.

"I'm helping that woman down the alley," I said, pointing in her direction. Nothing could be seen — the man must have pulled her out of sight. My self-appointed guard started to walk toward me. I took two fast steps back for each long stride he took forward.

A siren wailed. Clearly it was headed our way. The guard jerked his head back at the other men, his gun swinging away from my face. I exhaled. One of the men yelled, "Get inside!" All five of them ran for the door, more guns appearing from inside their jumpsuits, as the first police car pulled up.

"This way!" I shouted at the two officers. They didn't even look my way, stationing themselves behind their car and aiming their own guns at the boarded-up building. The few intact window panes shattered from inside. I pictured the five men jostling for position for an imminent shootout. I dropped to the ground and froze.

"Come out with your hands up," one cop said through a bullhorn. More sirens could be heard in the distance, headed toward us.

Looking around carefully, I realized I was out of the line of fire, out of both of their lines of attention. Down the alley where the couple had disappeared, a tennis shoe lay in the gravel where it hadn't been before. Forcing regular breaths, I got up and walked rapidly toward the woman, trying not to look like a running target, glancing all the while back at the pending shootout behind me.

No shots rang out. I could think about what was ahead of me again, not worry about a shot from the back. I continued to take deep breaths in an even pattern.

A man in a white T-shirt and jeans took off running from the doorway. "Stop!" I yelled, looked back to see how far away I was from the line of fire, and ran after him. He glanced back at me and I caught a look at his deeply tanned, lined face — white male, medium height and build, brown crew cut, clean-shaven, a little younger than me. More sirens were headed our way. He ran faster.

For a few days short of age fifty, I'm in good shape, and my six feet in height and morning jogs helped me keep up for a minute. But I lost him in a condo parking lot as he weaved and ducked among the cars and fled in an unseen direction.

Where were the cops? Vainly I scanned the alley for an officer on foot behind me, so that I could at least point out where I'd last seen the man.

Nobody! In sheer frustration I loped back to the woman in the alley. She still lay there, apparently passed out. Where was Kitt? The woman didn't seem to be going anywhere, so before I checked on her condition I eased toward the street to look for Kitt.

She was huddled behind her Viper. "Kitt!" I said.

"Shh, get down, it's some kind of bust," she whispered. "And you thought I was joking about the place being a drug lab!"

I squatted beside her. "I saw the men run inside. Have the cops gone in yet?" I strained to see something and kept my voice low. A dumpster was in my way. Kitt had a better vantage point around the front fender.

"Hell, yes, it's all over now, but I'm not taking any chances. When all the backup cars started to arrive, the five guys came out with their hands up. Nobody fired a shot. They're lined up out in the street. They're being handcuffed and shoved into the police cars." She paused for another moment. "Okay, they're being driven off. A few cops are going inside to check it out. It's probably okay to get up now — nothing's happened for a few minutes. What did you find out?"

I told her of the escape, and of the unconscious woman needing our attention.

"We'd better get back there. Officer!" Kitt shouted at one of the remaining policemen. "There's a woman who needs help back here in the alley — that's why I called you in the first place. Can someone take care of her?" She rubbed gravel from her knees.

Looking annoyed, the closest officer relayed a message to another policeman on the scene before joining us.

"What seems to be the problem here?" he asked. "You say you're the one who called police? We're going to need a statement."

"It can wait — didn't you hear, somebody needs help?" I glared at him. He glared back. Typical L.A. police–community relations. Still, I was grateful for how quickly they'd arrived this time. His reluctance showing, he followed us, using a handkerchief to wipe his bare shiny head, fringed by a friar's circle of dark blond.

All three of us reached the hidden doorway where we could hear moans before we could see the matted, waist-length, dull brown hair covering her dirty face, the wrinkled and stained yellow T-shirt, the pale, scrawny bare legs leading up to her wet brown triangle, the heap of faded denim and dingy cotton twisted around her foot. Her vacuous expression gave no hint of her age; she could have been thirty or fifty.

I knelt and took the woman in my arms and brushed her hair away. She smelled of alcohol as well as sweat, and I noticed an empty bottle of wine near her discarded clothes. She grabbed for her underpants and jeans and covered herself. Kitt brought her the tennis shoe from the alley. Another shoe was under the bottle.

"*Hayley?*" Kitt asked, her dark eyes opening wide.

"You know this woman? Hayley who, ma'am?" the officer said, taking out a notebook from his shirt pocket.

"I don't know what you're talking about. My name is Allison," the tear-streaked face insisted, her words slurring like a slow-motion playback of overly perfect diction. Her eyes were a chilly blue-gray and her shoulders went rigid as she pushed my comforting away. "Get away from me," she ordered.

"Ma'am, I have to know what happened. Were you raped?" the officer asked.

"NO! That was my boyfriend. You have no right to be here. So leave me alone." She overpronounced each syllable.

She cursed and swept gravel from under her hips and tried to maneuver herself into her underpants while keeping the jeans over her nakedness.

The cop looked at both of us and shrugged. "You heard the lady. You two have any evidence to the contrary?" He wrinkled his nose, telling me the smell of alcohol — and body odor — had reached him. Just another street person, I bet he was thinking.

I was sure she'd been fighting this guy, and he'd run off like someone who was guilty. But the woman repeated, "Get out of here!"

"You heard the lady," the officer said again. "You didn't see what you thought." Nodding at Kitt, he added, "You, the one who called nine-one-one, you have to make that statement."

Screwing up her face in frustration, Kitt started to follow him, then turned to whisper to me, "Stay here with her till I get back, and don't let her get away." In an even lower voice she said, "That's Hayley Malone, the sixties rock star."

CHAPTER TWO

"Go away!" Hayley/Allison repeated, struggling with her jeans, stumbling in the gravel.

"Please, stay here a minute until Kitt gets back," I begged her. "It's okay, we want to help you. If you don't want to talk to the cops, that's okay. You're going to be okay, Hayley."

"I tell you, I'm Allison Chambers." She made as if to leave.

"Okay, Allison, please, if you need help, just talk to me. My name's Laney Samms, and my friend is Kitt Meyers. Do you remember her? She knows you.

She's your friend. She'll be back in just a second. While we were trying to reach you, there was some kind of arrest around the corner." Trying to kill time until Kitt came back, I explained to her what had happened. I talked slowly, taking my time, using a calming tone of voice, keeping her from bolting. "What a coincidence, huh? But that's L.A. for you."

She broke loose from my arm and started walking down the alley. I didn't want to immobilize her against her will; she had to be traumatized already. I walked along, getting in her way, trying to slow her down if not stop her.

"Is there someplace special you're going? I can drive you in that great-looking red sports car back there," I offered. She glanced back but kept on walking. I tried telepathy again to signal Kitt to hurry.

"Ouch!" Hayley/Allison reached down to remove her left shoe and shake out a chunk of gravel. She looked around as if suddenly realizing she didn't know where she was. "What street is that?" she asked, gesturing in the direction of the car.

I racked my brain. Funny, the things you don't pay attention to. "Uh, I never noticed, but Santa Monica Boulevard is right around the corner, and we're a couple blocks from Robertson, the nearest major cross street. We're in West Hollywood." I couldn't tell if she recognized the city. "Los Angeles. California. Where are you going?"

She looked stunned. Turning slowly, she looked all around her. "How did I get here?" she muttered.

"Look, let me take you to Kitt's office where you can wash your face and we can help you figure out what to do next. How about it?"

Luckily, Kitt arrived before the woman could decide which direction to go this time. "Hayley, I'm glad I found you. Do you remember me, Kitt Meyers? It was, what, nineteen seventy-six when you were living in Shell House and my folks got you on Johnny Carson?"

Hayley let herself be taken in Kitt's arms. Her body went limp. Kitt hung onto her with my help until she could straighten her legs again. The grimace on Hayley's face when Kitt mentioned the Carson show made me positive she didn't want to remember that episode. And vaguely I remembered the disastrous comeback attempt. Yes, this woman was Hayley Malone.

I recalled the naïve seventeen-year-old who'd sung an idealistic duet with Stevie Wonder after the 1967 Detroit riots. She was an open wound singing about how her home — a flat above a liquor store — burned down during the uprising and how the world needed racial harmony because we're all hurting. I think it was the first time I'd heard someone say racism hurts whites too. From the mouths of babes.

Hayley was a pale-eyed innocent child, whose straight mouse-brown hair fell like angel wings around her face and whose voice sounded like a soloist in a Viennese boys' choir. I remembered a disc jockey of the period who loved to play The Doors' sexually charged "Light My Fire," then the black power message of "Burn, Baby, Burn," then the plaintive "We're All Hurting," as a full emotional circle on the theme.

I also remembered reading that Hayley's mother, rumored to have been highly protective of her innocent daughter, died shortly after that song, and how Hayley shocked the world when she seemed to grow up overnight on her eighteenth birthday.

She proved it with a blatantly sexual album cover featuring her full breasts overflowing a black leather bustier, hips straining her black leather bell-bottoms cut low to show off her navel and small waist. Her voice — and lyrics — were no longer sweet.

"Another Janis Joplin," critics had raved. When Janis overdosed, it seemed that Hayley's career plummeted as well — the public could tolerate only so much pain, and it appeared inevitable that Hayley would come to the same end.

Last I'd heard, Hayley had been in and out of a few cults, tried the Betty Ford Center a couple of times, and attempted that pathetic comeback on the Carson show à la Tiny Tim tiptoeing through pitiful tulips.

Kitt helped Hayley walk to her office building, where she used a key to get in the back door. I half-carried her up the flight of stairs and into Kitt's offices. She collapsed on the plaid sofa. Kitt ran her fingertips over Hayley's forehead while I brought a can of apple juice from Kitt's fridge.

"Can I wash up?" Hayley asked abruptly. "Do you have a shower?"

"I do," Kitt said in a soothing voice. "But first, I need to ask you one question. If you were raped, we need to take you to a hospital so you can get some medical attention. You shouldn't shower first."

"I told you, I wasn't raped!"

"So who was that guy, and why didn't he stick around?" I asked.

"He . . . he's my ghost." Defiance was in her voice.

Kitt and I stared at her and at each other.

"I told you, he's a ghost. He shows up every so often. Usually nobody else sees him. He's a ghost. It didn't mean anything. It wasn't rape, I tell you."

Kitt took me aside and whispered, "She's delusional. She needs help."

I nodded. "Do we take her to a hospital?"

"I don't know, I worry about the publicity. They'll ship her to Camarillo for observation and nobody deserves that. All she needs is to have her photo on the front page looking like a bag lady. Let me think." In a normal voice, she said, "Hayley, what do you think about the idea of going back to the Betty Ford Center?"

"Yes!" Hayley shouted. "I'm safe there. Yes! Take me to Betty Ford!" She actually smiled. I could see now it was definitely Hayley Malone. And she was still beautiful.

"It costs a lot of money. Will you cover it?" I went back to a whisper to Kitt.

"I heard that — I've got medical insurance. What day is it?" Hayley interrupted.

"What?" we both responded.

"What day is it? Is it past June first yet?"

We nodded.

"Then money's not a problem. I get my money the first of every month. I've got enough to pay for the clinic even if the insurance won't pay this time. Please, please get me to Betty Ford's." Hope shone in her smudged eyes.

"How many times have you been there already?" I asked. They had to have limits.

"Uh, three, I think, but they'll take me back. I

know they will." She looked around the office for a phone. Kitt made the call, turning away and cupping the receiver so that we couldn't hear her words.

"They'll take her," she announced. "Look, my car only seats two. Laney, can you stay here, call somebody to come get you, arrange something?"

"Sure." I ran through a list of possibilities. Actually I could catch the bus to where Santa Monica ends at Sunset and walk down Hyperion the few blocks to Samms', the bar I own in Silverlake. "Just get her to the clinic." To Hayley I said, "I'm sorry we met this way, but I want you to know that you gave me a lot of enjoyment when you were singing. I have a lot of great memories of you." I smiled for her, while wondering inside what in the world could have happened to the superstar.

Raped by a ghost. The wetness on her crotch where he'd pulled out hadn't been imaginary. I tried to keep his nondescript face in my mind for future reference, in case he was ever caught.

CHAPTER THREE

The cops told Kitt to beef up whatever security measures she had at her home and office, in case partners of the guys they'd arrested tracked us down. Of course they couldn't provide any security themselves; they didn't even have enough officers to stop crimes in process, much less guard individuals against only potential violence. Reassuring.

"This probably won't get to trial, but if it does you may have to testify," an officer told us. We really looked forward to that event.

So for the next few weeks Kitt's attorney kept

checking and found that the guys plea-bargained for sentences ranging from five to ten years on assorted charges, such as possession of drug paraphernalia (not to mention that the "paraphernalia" was the complete innards of a designer drug manufacturing plant). We spent an uneasy period jumping at sudden sounds until the danger seemed to have passed. Even after the news of the plea bargaining, I couldn't help looking around more often, staring at innocent strangers.

Kitt kept up with Hayley's progress, visiting her several weekends at Betty Ford's, bringing her clothes and toiletries. She told me that Hayley decided to spend two months at the clinic instead of the usual one, on the recommendation of the doctors, and that this time she was really determined to kick her addictions.

With all of Kitt's involvement, I suppose I shouldn't have been surprised the day in late August when I got the phone call from her at the desert hospital.

"How is she?" I asked.

"She's doing fine, and this time she thinks she'll make it," Kitt said, hesitating.

"Good for her," I said absentmindedly, then suddenly woke up to the fact that Kitt was not making idle conversation.

"Look, Laney, I have a big favor to ask..."

I braced myself.

"Hayley really doesn't have anyplace else to go now, and she needs a safe, secure environment, with someone who understands alcoholism."

I saw it coming.

"I'll be gone over Labor Day on that Robin Tyler

cruise to the Bahamas, and since you're going to all those AA meetings anyway ..."

"Where is she going to stay, Kitt?" I asked, as if I didn't know.

"The guest suite. I've got lots of room at the house, and it's kind of out of the way of temptation ..."

"If she really wanted to get drugs or alcohol she could hike down to Figueroa," I reminded her.

"I know that, but at least the stuff won't be in her face ... and she'll have someone around who knows what she's going through ..." Kitt was waiting to hear my reaction.

It was mixed. Secretly I'm no different from the fans who try to get autographs of famous celebrities, and I read the *Enquirer* headlines while in line at the grocery. One of the perks of working for Kitt Meyers is meeting the figures in the women's music industry in real life. Part of me was dying for the chance to meet Hayley Malone in person, now that she was sober again and presumably nondelusional.

The last story I'd read about her in one of her streaks of sobriety had described her as Lauren Bacall meets Madonna.

The story had added, when she was drinking it was John Wayne meets Tweetie Bird.

The rest of me would rather die than deal with another recovering alcoholic twenty-four hours a day, especially since I'd been sober for a year. Twenty years, if you didn't count that one disastrous binge over Rhonda Rasmussen. It counted.

"If I wanted to be a psych tech I'd apply at Camarillo," I told Kitt.

"I know, I know, but you're better than a lot of

21

people she could get hooked up with. She's got nowhere else to go. She'll get the support she needs with us. What do you say? You've got nothing major coming down in your life the next few weeks."

"Thanks a lot," I grimaced. So what if it was true.

"So you'll do it?" When Kitt was excited, sometimes her voice rose to the stratosphere. The "it" drifted off into the clouds.

"Do what, exactly? Spell 'it' out," I demanded.

"Just hang around with her some, be there for her, take her to your AA meetings for the next couple of weeks, maybe take in a few extra meetings. You can do it. You'll be great."

Kitt was born persuading; she was a "red-diaper baby" born to two Jewish left-wing radicals whose goal was nothing short of improving the entire world. Her father's father fought in the Spanish Civil War with every other leftist American male who could get there; her grandmother actually knew Emma Goldman and all those people in the movie *Reds*.

Her father and mother had become lawyers for social activists and found themselves defending Hollywood entertainers during the McCarthy era and afterward and getting rich in the process. Kitt used the contacts from her childhood well in her women's music dealings.

"Forget flattery," I told her. "Say, why are you so interested in continuing to take care of Hayley? Don't tell me Hayley Malone is a dyke who's going to be the next great lesbian heartthrob?"

Kitt's silence was the answer.

"Kitt . . . you know how recovery goes. You can't

count on a thing. And who says she's a lesbian anyway? What about that supposed boyfriend? The rumors I've always heard had her fucking anything that moved."

"She's been mostly with women since her Shell House days, in the mid-seventies when I first met her."

A thought hit me. "Kitt, are you trying to get in tight with her so she'll bring some money your way if she makes a comeback?"

"Laney! How can you say that?"

I let the pause grow pregnant.

"Yeah, the thought entered my mind. But say nothing comes of it, she uses me, us, and splits, so what, we've done our bit to help a sister in need. You're so . . . cynical, Laney."

"Experienced, that's the word you're looking for."

"So, she still needs help, and she needs someone exactly like you, all right?" Kitt let her argument rest there, while I shifted the phone back and forth between ears.

All I could think of was the last time I'd seen Hayley Malone in person when she was on top. Somebody had dragged me to San Francisco for one of those April or November Mobilizations Against the War that went on for years in the late sixties and early seventies. Hayley had been on the speakers' platform, performing between speeches by Angela Davis and Coretta King, to keep people awake despite their contact highs.

A peacock, maybe two, had died for her outfit, unless those feathers had been shed naturally one by one, but, hey, who cared about animal rights in those days? A full cape of iridescent feathers draped around her shoulders like Icarus's wings, fastened to her wrists with beaded leather bracelets, waved in the wind and fluttered across a barely there turquoise leather bra.

Otherwise, she had on only a turquoise leather miniskirt, slit high on each hip, and supple, beaded calf-high leather boots on her bare, tanned legs. As she strutted, the muscles in her thighs rippled like an Amazon's. If she was cold, she gave no sign, swigging from her trademark bottle of cherry wine. Her hair was no longer the seventeen-year-old's ironed-straight mousy brown but a tawny mane of many colors. A turquoise and scarlet lightning design zigzagged down her cheeks and thighs.

She sang of revolution, of peace, of war, of fighting back against the government, against Nixon, and even sometimes of love. All the great clichés of the late sixties and early seventies. And something behind her pale eyes had yanked my soul despite itself.

I wondered if anybody else at the demonstration had been thinking the same mixed thoughts — this very young, strong, strutting woman on the outside, whose voice cried out for an end to the war, an end to injustice, could use some real loving, some real caring, on the inside. I wondered if anyone else suspected that they were exactly the right person to do the loving. Hayley had had that effect back then, the same way Marilyn Monroe had affected audiences the decade before.

I shook myself back into the present. So now was my chance to give that sixties waif the caring she needed then. Better late than never. Besides, I'd gotten into trouble before by drifting too far away from AA, by forgetting the twelfth step.

I had almost managed to convince myself it was my civic duty to take care of Hayley. Whatever the Hayley of the nineties had become.

"What kind of shape is Hayley in now?" I had to ask. "Does she look better than she did when we found her?"

Kitt snorted. "What do you think? She's been through hell. She's skinny, her complexion is sallow . . . oh, and she's bald."

"Bald!" I couldn't visualize it. She *had* to have her tawny hair falling in her face so that she could shake her whole body and make it fly. Hayley wouldn't be Hayley without all that hair.

"Yeah, she shaved her head this morning, says it's a symbol of her finally breaking away from everything in her past, a starting over. Don't stare too hard at her white scalp, okay? She's got a lot of fresh razor cuts all over her head."

I couldn't help smiling. It sounded like something a drunk would do on the spur of the moment and regret it later. Then I sighed. Judging from her past record, she wouldn't last long sober. She wasn't going to need anything too difficult. Make sure she gets up in the morning, eats something, gets some exercise, goes to meetings, talks about whatever is on her zapped mind . . . I could handle it. I used to babysit as a kid.

"How did the rape affect her?" I asked.

"She acts like it didn't happen. Says she's been raped before, it's no big deal."

That response horrified me. I'd always thought

that if I was about to be raped, I'd rather die than let it happen. I'd fight back with every breath in me. I took rape self-defense training from Betty Brooks at Cal State Long Beach and practiced every move as if my life depended on it.

But then I'd met women who said they'd felt like me and instead they'd gone passive when a violent rape actually happened. I couldn't blame Hayley for her life choices. All I could do was offer help.

"Okay, okay, I'll do it. But remember, it's not my fault if she splits."

"Whew, thanks a lot, Laney, I owe you big. We'll be home in a couple of hours, and I'll get pizza, okay?"

"Where at?"

"I have to stop at Tower Records on Ventura first. I got them to stock Dos Fallopia's 'My Breasts Are Out of Control' and Dobkin's 'Love & Politics: A Thirty-Year Saga.' Now they're trying to back out because somebody complained."

"You're coming from the valley? Barone's, then — double cheese with everything, including anchovies." My mouth watered at the thought.

"Not that crap!"

"You owe me big," I reminded her.

"Okay, I'll get two, one for you with the fish. And Laney, thanks again."

"I get a feeling I'm going to regret this," I said, but Kitt had already hung up. The phone rang again almost instantly.

"Laney? It's still Kitt. I have another favor to ask — can you go into my bedroom and look through my underwear drawers? I think I have a lid of sinsemilla somewhere, if it didn't get stolen in the last burglary. Throw the whole bag down the garbage disposal, okay?"

"What!"

"I'm sorry, I shouldn't have had it around when you were recovering, but I didn't think marijuana was your thing, and besides, you'd never go through my underwear anyway."

"I read someplace it's the first place burglars look. Okay, okay, I'll get rid of it if I find it." I let my voice show my annoyance.

"I haven't smoked anything for years. The stuff's probably no good anymore." She tried to defend herself, then gave up. "Look, I said I'm sorry. Just help me through this. It could be really important."

"And then again you might get ripped off royally, and so might I," I warned her. "Check on your insurance, and, hey, remember the anchovies."

I could hear Kitt's relief through the phone. "See ya soon," she said. "Oh, and by the way, I called the security guards to put the extra watch back on the house again, just on general principles." She always did when she had a celebrity staying with her.

"Good idea," I responded as she hung up.

I let myself remember Hayley in peacock blue.

CHAPTER FOUR

When I hung up and left the guesthouse for the main building, heat radiated from the ground as if a forest fire had just swept through. What else could I expect, it was late August, a lazy Monday. Visible waves of heat undulated from Mount Washington side- walks, even though we're high above northeast L.A. and usually cooled by breezes when the rest of the city stagnates.

Most of the homes on Mount Washington were built in the 1920s as summer resorts for wealthy city dwellers who lived what was then a long ways away, nearer downtown L.A. Today, when L.A.'s "suburbs" radiate a hundred miles, Mount Washington is considered practically downtown L.A. itself.

The breathtaking view from Kitt's second story reveals a solid pattern of houses and hills as far as the eye can see — but only on the rare clear day, after a rain or stiff wind. The Pacific trails along the far western horizon like a taffeta ribbon.

Kitt likes to sit on the balcony with her cordless phone and make her business calls to the world below. I took a second to look for the view before searching for her grass, but the smog clamped in layers like a muddy Singapore Sling over the landscape.

Shoved far in the back of her bra drawer, behind a black lace number I never dreamed Kitt would own — but then, maybe she kept it on hand for lovers to dress up in — I found Kitt's marijuana baggie and ground it up in the disposal. The time I first choked on it and knew it wasn't my main thing, the stuff probably cost ten or fifteen dollars; now it must be worth twenty times more.

Though Kitt made a point of not having any alcohol around in case it might tempt me, I checked all the likely spots anyway. The house was clean. Just like me. Thank you, HP. One more day at a time. It wasn't a cliché if I didn't say it aloud.

Outside, the yellow plaid, plastic-webbed aluminum lawn chair squeaked when I sank down in the shade of Kitt Meyers' guesthouse and waited for her to arrive with Hayley Malone.

I debated changing my white cutoffs and red

Toshi Reagon T-shirt to something spiffier but decided that would be ridiculous, considering her probable state. Bald. I had to chuckle.

My white German shepherd eyed the pool longingly but I tapped her long muzzle in warning. "We don't have many rules here, Radar, but keeping you out of the pool is one of them." She whimpered but obeyed.

Next Monday was Labor Day, and the day after that my fiftieth birthday. No longer did the number choke in my throat. Forty-nine had been horrid, but I'd resisted middle age long enough. Fifty was fine. Maybe they'd have a party down at the bar. What would Anne be doing, I mused in remorse for the thousandth time since my stupidity had led to our final breakup a year and a half ago.

No, it wasn't my fault. We'd just settled into a bad kind of relationship where I was stagnating, and I'd had to wrench myself free, at tremendous cost. Anne had loving parents who lived in Sonoma, a son and new daughter-in-law at Stanford, and a new veterinary tech in Silverlake who probably coveted her boss's body.

"And what do you and I have, Radar, hmm?" I surveyed the two-acre, wood-fenced estate — in L.A. a few acres in a nice neighborhood qualifies as an estate.

Both the sprawling two-story main house and the guesthouse I live in are a cool beige stucco with cinnamony brick-colored Spanish tile roofs. Flaming fuschia bougainvillea threatened to bury both buildings. A few feet from me was the barbecue, red cedar gazebo and hot tub. L.A. heaven — Kitt had arrived. Even if the estate didn't belong to me, I had to admit it was a nice place to live.

Being Kitt's house sitter takes almost no time. Besides making sure the gardener, pool maintenance crew and housecleaner do their jobs and taking care of her assorted cats, now and then I drive to the airport to pick up a celebrity or deliver an emergency order to a music store or concert. I put out a newsletter on my laptop computer for her best customers and music stores, to tell them of upcoming events.

For this I get free rent, a small salary, and an occasional bonus for extraordinary duties. Kitt hadn't mentioned any extra money for babysitting Hayley. So it was *pro bono*.

I've got plenty of time to check on Samms', the bar in Silverlake I had jointly owned with Anne for twenty years and which now was wholly mine, under Carmen's great management. We're surviving the recession fairly well — people still have to have someplace to unwind and be among friends and let off steam and, yes, cruise, all for the price of a beer or two. At least the economic downturn has caused the land developers to forget about attempting to turn the bar and all of Hyperion into another strip mall.

I do a little public relations work on the side for some other Silverlake gay and lesbian small businesses and organizations, and I'm on the board again for AIDS Aid, the only community organization I totally support because somehow we've kept politics out of the day-to-day work of helping people.

I don't miss all the other groups for which Anne

and I had served on the boards, back when I was willing to follow her around and live out her life's dreams while never discovering my own. I was her tall, silver-haired escort in the tuxedo to all the fancy benefits. I'd left the tuxedo behind when I moved out.

Overall, my life is in order, even though I still don't have my own dream. Maybe this was it — my own version of a dream life. Could be.

So I'm lonely sometimes, despite all the people who come through Kitt's house. So I'm a few days short of fifty and alone. So what? Compared to ninety-nine percent of the world, I'm living the high life.

"We've got it made, Radar," I said, scratching her ears. She moaned in gratitude and leaned into my hand. Or did she need ear mite drops?

The wrought-iron gate to the outside world groaned and swung open, the garage door followed suit, and Kitt's Viper drove in and parked. The garage door strained downward.

"Hi, Laney." Kitt arrived at the pool wearing one of those natural, safari-style cotton pants-and-jacket outfits in a pale green that set off her deep olive skin.

The suit was wrinkled, but then Kitt herself always is, not quite groomed no matter how much she spends on good clothes. When she smiles her deep dimples and laugh lines make her face match her outfits. But like a massive English sheepdog, if you try to push her against her will, she's an immovable force under that lovable shaggy exterior.

If I were a dog — well, Radar would be my twin.

The shadow that had to be Hayley was in an

oversized white shirt over baggy denim cutoffs. Above her Birkenstocks, her thin legs were as pale as her scalp. She'd be a greyhound, too worn out for the racetrack anymore. *Sleek* is a nicer word than *skinny*, *alert* nicer than *jumpy*.

"You remember Hayley Malone," Kitt said. Was there anxiety in her voice?

"Yes, of course." I got up from my lawn chair, trying to get a glimpse of the singer's face.

"I'm grateful to be here, really," Hayley said in a surprisingly strong voice, shifting forward enough to show herself.

What would you look like if you'd been on a bad trip for twenty years? That's how she looked, a sallow-complected skeleton with that pale, bald, razor-marked scalp glistening like a scratched chrome bumper. But she stood straight and tall, and as she met my gaze she shook her shorn head as if she still had the tawny streaked mane to throw around.

"I must still look a mess, but I look a whole lot better than when you saw me last." The throaty voice had a definite edge of resiliency, not the high-pitched whine of the alley episode. Hayley took a step forward, moving as quickly and gracefully as the greyhound I'd imagined her to be. Her eyes were pale gray-blue, like ice cubes melting at the bottom of a weak drink.

I remembered those ice-cold eyes piercing me and a quarter-million other people in Golden Gate Park at another, later anti-war rally. We could have all taken flight on the fumes in the air, and Hayley's expression was out of it by then. She'd gone through the motions, and did she have motions! But she'd seemed to be on automatic pilot. I remembered wondering back then if she was all right, if maybe she was in deep trouble.

We didn't care. We were all in trouble, the world was in trouble, we might as well dance away the days and nights like Poe's revelers defying the Black Plague. I'd been a little high myself, on Kahlúa and homegrown provided by the woman who'd dragged me there, one of the nameless, faceless women of that period of my life. I shook away the memories.

Hayley and Kitt were standing there, waiting for me to say something.

"I'm very happy to see you again, Hayley." I finally could talk.

"What do you think of my hair?" Hayley asked outright, touching her scalp. Her eyes no longer looked like ice cubes but like heather mist.

I feigned shock. "Do you need a few Band-Aids?"

Her eyes crinkled and she let out a short chuckle. "Ha! I like you, Laney. We're going to get along just fine," she said, letting the twinkle remain in her eyes. "And your hair's gorgeous — premature?"

"It used to be," I said, smiling back. "Some people still call me Silver. It's Priscilla Elaine Samms. Through the years I got called Priscilly, Silly, Sil, Silver, Sam, Laney . . . I'll answer to just about anything."

Kitt grasped her firmly by the elbow. "Come on, I want you to see your room and the rest of the joint and then we can get settled. Laney, would you get the pizza from the car and bring it into the kitchen? Hayley, I hope you're hungry, this is the best pizza in L.A."

She compared favorite pizza haunts with Hayley as she steered the singer back into the main house.

"No way — they use *canned mushrooms* !" I heard Kitt argue. "How about the Chicago Pizza Factory?" Their voices faded.

Radar padded alongside me, putting in her bid in advance for the crust of my last slice. The pizza smelled heavenly. I threw some romaine lettuce and tomato slices in a bowl and called it salad, laid out Kitt's best stoneware, and poured Diet Pepsi for myself.

"Lemonade from real lemons, iced tea, a couple kinds of soft drinks. What's your choice?" I asked when they joined me.

I poured them both lemonade and we sat down to devour the two thick-crust, square-pan pizzas, one with pepperoni only, the other my favorite.

"I've got to gain some weight back, so you'd better take what you want now — the rest is mine!" Hayley announced. Kitt stuck out her tongue.

Hayley liked my pizza better than Kitt's, a mixed pleasure. Radar barely got one crust from me, though she snitched almost all of Hayley's last slice.

"Phew, all three of you stink of anchovies," Kitt said, holding her nose. She put her leftovers in the fridge for breakfast.

Hayley gave a lot of attention to Radar, who was in love. I watched Hayley's hand sneak under the table to scratch Radar's ears.

"Good dog!" Hayley's voice was muffled by the ruff of white hair as she bent down to hug Radar. Pets are good therapy, I reminded myself. Hayley needs this. Still, I was a little jealous. So much for my bragging rights to my one-woman canine. Radar is a pretty decent judge of character — Hayley passed her test. So maybe there was hope for her. She liked anchovies, didn't she?

Mentally I reviewed all the AA meetings I'd been to, trying to decide which would be the best for a celebrity, one where nobody would break AA anonymity and tell a tabloid where a quick photo could be taken.

"I have to leave tomorrow morning for Miami to work a cruise," Kitt continued. "I'll be back sometime next Tuesday or Wednesday. What were you going to do for Labor Day, Laney?"

I was going to be alone, of course. Oh, she wanted me to include Hayley, try to put something together. So much for my moping. Maybe this was going to be good therapy for me as well as for Hayley.

"I'll make a few calls, see if somebody is having an extended family picnic that can extend a bit more. Hayley, I know some great cooks. Did Kitt tell you I own a bar? Great occupation for a recovering alcoholic, right, but I did it for twenty years with no trouble. Then I ran into the wrong woman, and I blew it. Big time." I didn't look at her when I said this, still unnerved by the Rhonda Rasmussen episode. "But I got back in AA and got myself together again. I just had my one-year cake a few weeks ago. I leave the bar in the hands of Carmen, my manager, most of the time. I'll call her, see what's going on with some of the old gang."

"Clean and sober?" Hayley's mouth had a wry twist, almost mocking the overworked phrase.

"Natch."

Kitt stood up and stretched. "It's still pretty warm. Anybody for a swim to work off the pizza?"

Radar barked.

"Not you, silly dog. I've got a couple extra suits — one's bound to fit you, Hayley. Everybody except Radar into the pool!"

"Umm," Hayley said, remaining in her chair as Kitt headed for her room. She looked at me quizzically. "Who needs suits? We're all going to be family for a few weeks, right?" Kitt stopped mid-step and turned, looking first at Hayley, then at me. I shrugged my shoulders.

With a knowing smile, Hayley asked, "Don't tell me you'd wear suits if I weren't here."

"Uh, no," Kitt admitted.

Hayley stood up and pulled off her shirt in one motion. Too-thin is back in — models kill themselves dieting trying to look that slim. Somehow her breasts were still full, though her ribs were like ladder rungs when she lifted her arms. Implants? No, she'd been big-breasted at eighteen — who could forget that album cover? Her waist was as tiny as Vivian Leigh's in *Gone With the Wind*, though those hips wouldn't hold up her old hip-huggers. Would she have gotten so far in her career without that body, no matter how plaintive and powerful her voice?

I kept being drawn to her breasts while trying not to stare. Her small nipples were a deep rose against her pale beige skin, the narrow pink areolas like tiny halos. My breath caught.

Hayley grinned at me, apparently knowing the effect her sudden strip had on me. "So which way's the pool?"

Kitt and I looked at each other again. "This way," I said, peeling off my own T-shirt as I walked. Kitt brought up the rear, skipping on one foot as she tugged off her green slacks.

Hayley strolled to the edge of the pool like Madonna in her "Vogue" video, her sideways glance indicating she was highly aware of her audience of two. "Umm, love the smell of chlorine." Strange thing to say, I thought. She walked to the deep end, then did a quick jackknife and came up shrieking, "It's not heated!"

"It's August!" Kitt yelled back. She sat on the edge and let her feet dangle. "It's not that cool to me. You just need to get some meat on those bones."

Some of us jump right into a new adventure, others of us take it a little slower. Kitt took her time. I cannonballed in, my splash causing more shouts from Hayley. She tried to dunk me in retaliation, pushing hard on my shoulders in a fast jab that caught me unawares and left my mouth full of water. Was this her version of flirting? I caught myself wondering.

"So you want to play, hey?" I sputtered. "You have been warned!" My foot caught behind her knee and dragged her under first. I liked being near this woman. And I knew better than to let myself like it too much. I was no amateur at her games, but this woman had her Ph.D. in sexology.

She disappeared underwater and, while I was looking for her, she came up behind me and tugged me backwards by my hair. I came up gasping. We chased each other around the pool, Radar racing around the rim after us, barking at our shouts.

"Time out. I'm exhausted!" Hayley said, paddling to the ladder and hanging on the steps, gasping and rubbing water from her eyes. I did a few laps in the Australian crawl while Kitt worked her way into the water via the steps.

"It's warm, Kitt!" I responded. "Just jump in!"

She finally slid her whole body under, pausing when the ripples hit her nipples. Neither Kitt nor I are abundantly endowed, but I couldn't help noticing that the water made all of us look our best. Lecher, I told myself, still trying not to stare at Hayley.

I pulled myself up onto the edge of the pool and tickled Radar's muzzle as Hayley competed with Kitt on a butterfly stroke race of two laps. Kitt won; Hayley was winded. She looked dejected over the silly loss.

"The butterfly is Kitt's best stroke," I had to call out to Hayley to make her feel better.

"I prefer the breast stroke myself," she retorted, with a sly glance at me. "I've got to get back in shape." I bit my lip to avoid saying the obvious sexist rejoinder.

"Just takes time," Kitt reassured her. "By the way, in case you two aren't up when I leave, have a good weekend, and I'll see you next week. I'm turning in early." She left. The screened rear security door slammed.

Hayley momentarily had that look of a child lost in a department store. She caught herself.

"I'll be fine, don't worry about me," she said. "You're going to be around the whole time, right?" She looked pointedly in my direction.

"Uh huh."

She nodded, then yawned. "I'm real tired. Think I'll hit the sack early too." She used the ladder to get out of the pool when her attempt to hoist herself up on the side failed.

She gave Radar another hug after she dried off, burying her head in the dog's ruff like a child in her mother's lap.

"Look, Laney, would you mind if Radar slept with me tonight? I kind of think I'd like to have a warm body in the room with me. If it's okay."

"Sure," I said agreeably, hiding my jealousy. "If she'll come with you. She's a one-woman dog."

As if to prove me wrong, Radar followed Hayley to her bedroom. Traitor, I sent the dog a message by telepathy.

And then I was alone by the pool. My body was tingly from the horseplay with Hayley. I knew I couldn't sleep. But I had just the solution: Joanie.

I turned on the hot tub and, when it was warm, slid in. Was it watching Hayley strip off her clothes which had put me in the mood? These days I was monogamous with the water jet that bubbled furiously from the back of the seat on the right side.

By sitting just so, I could get the jet stream to rush across my labia and hit right at my clitoris.

Forcing all detritus from my mind, I concentrated on the flow of the water over me. We are creatures of the sea, I sometimes thought, and should have never come on land. Lovely, warm, soothing water. The jet stream pulsated against me and I squirmed on the seat to get the fullest effect. My fingers went to my nipples and I turned off the world.

I let myself drift through time. Soon I was dancing to an ever-more-frantic drumbeat, Mardi Gras revelers reaching out for me, their fingers the ones on my breasts. I romped in ocean waves, fell into the swirling tide, glided through warm water on a playful dolphin whose rubbery fin tickled my labia, rode the surf on a horse with the saddle beating up against me, nuzzled a golden woman who was touching me just so.

I was lying on fine white sand on the shore where the waves lapped at my body, rolling over and over with the woman who kept her strong hand in place as we kissed and strained against our feverish urges. We gave in to our bodies' surging pulsations, and somehow we flew away on a swirling waterspout that carried us without effort through the sky.

Suddenly we were falling, plunging toward a giant Italian fountain that captured us, bounced us lightly in the air as if we were dancing cubes of Jello, pressed against our skin with strong pelts that somehow kept us floating in air throughout eons of time while the water pummeled every inch of our bodies.

We spun and twirled naked on the giant fountain until our bodies vibrated and we became one with the water, our bodies dissolving into an endless stream of the purest pleasures attuned to the eternal tides. The tide rolled in. The tide rolled out.

Seven minutes later, I was a quivering mass of protoplasm, all nerve endings unwound and hanging limp.

Thank you, Ms. Jett, for another wonderful evening. Now I could go to bed.

I still craved something else, preferably a woman to cuddle up to spoon-fashion. Too bad I quit smoking years ago. I drifted in the warm water until my breathing returned to normal. I'd have to watch it so I didn't fall asleep — too long in a hot tub can be harmful, I knew, though I didn't remember how.

"Hi."

My eyes shot open and I swung in the water to face the voice. Hayley posed in a halo of moonlight, her naked, slim body black against the clouds.

"Were you watching me?" I wasn't exactly annoyed.

"I plead guilty. Kitt may have planted trees so the neighbors can't see the pool, but I've got a clear shot at the hot tub from my window. I have to say, I enjoyed it almost as much as you did." She stepped into the water. "At least this is warm." She sniffed. "Chlorine's strong. Is there a particular jet that works best?"

I moved over from the molded fiberglass seat on the right. "Let me introduce you to Joanie — Ms. Joan Jett to you."

Hayley laughed, easing herself into place. "Joan

42

Jett, 'I Love Rock 'n Roll,' the rockers' anthem of the early eighties. I remember it well. She never did have another big hit. Ha, I should talk. The bubble gum and leather look turn you on, Laney?" She maneuvered her hips over the bubbling water. "Oh, yes, that's exactly right. Kitt must have had this jet special-made."

"She never said."

"And you never asked." Hayley chuckled. "Umm, this is good." She closed her eyes. "Excuse me if I pass on any further conversation for a few minutes."

"I'll leave —"

"Don't. Turnabout's fair. Unless it makes you uncomfortable?"

I didn't answer. The water level hit Hayley mid-chest. Her round breasts floated in the water, her nipples like tiny red bobbins announcing the presence of nibbling fish on the other end of a fishing pole. She touched her breasts, fingering the red buds like a child would caress her favorite cat's-eye marble. Her right hand reached down to her clitoris, amplifying the stimulation from the water.

Her left hand moved from nipple to nipple, seemingly wanting to be in both places at once.

Her eyes opened. She reached for my hands and placed them on her breasts, watching my face. I didn't pull back, though I debated it briefly.

She smiled, closed her eyes again, and went to work, hips wiggling against the water flow. Both of her hands disappeared below the water; I took both nipples and worked them lightly while Hayley came with a thrashing thrust that splashed water six feet around the patio. I held on, like clinging to the reins of a horse gone wild.

When her body quieted, she reached for me, her eyes still closed, and held me tightly while her breathing returned to normal. Her fingers clutched my skin as if I were a lifeguard. Her body was taut, so thin that there was no softness. My hands slipped on her skin as if she were made of Tupperware.

Still holding onto my shoulders with her arms, she began to move her lower body to join the pulsing of the water. I took her nipples once more and we moved together to help her reach a new climax. Almost immediately she went on to another, and another, rolling in the water like a cowboy taking an endurance test on a Brahman bull. I was enthralled. I felt as if I had known her all my life, as if she were a water nymph who'd been my shadow, dancing into view whenever I was alone and in the mood. The woman of my fantasies. The woman I'd had a crush on twenty-some years ago when she was a star.

When she rested, a limp heap on the molded seat, I shifted her sideways to another watery chair and took her place on Joanie. Hayley opened her eyes and reached out for my breasts. It was as if her hands were my own. I came instantly, already aroused almost to climax just from watching her. She laughed a throaty laugh and grabbed onto me and we hugged in the water, enjoying the last throes of our orgasms in the warm water until our bodies had quieted.

It was very still outside. Radar whimpered at us both. She put her paws up on the rim of the hot tub and licked first my face, then Hayley's. So it had been a foursome: Hayley, me, Joanie and Radar. I laughed quietly. I wondered briefly what Hayley's past included.

I remembered the face of the rapist in the alley.

Reality jolted me — I'd made love with a high-risk stranger.

No, we'd hugged and touched nipples, nothing could be safer than that. The chlorine was additional safety.

So I'd been a Hayley groupie for one night, I laughed to myself. Dreams do come true.

"Good night, Laney," she said, pulling away and easing herself out of the water. Dripping wet, she shook herself off. "Come on, Radar." And they were gone. Silence.

I let myself drift in the hot tub. What had just happened? Had it been a hallucination? Maybe I *had* spent too long in the hot water. I scrambled out of the tub and left wet footprints on the still-warm concrete on my way to the guesthouse.

I toweled off and stood there, debating. It was too warm to wear anything to bed. In fact, it was a night for air conditioning, something I use as little as possible. I climbed up the varnished pine ladder to the loft. The beach house has a bedroom but I'd made it into an office; Kitt stores her overflow of cassettes, CDs and promotional literature there as well. I sleep in the open loft over the small living room. Though the outside of the guesthouse is traditional California-Spanish, inside it's paneled like a pine log vacation cabin, a look I love.

Wrapping another towel over my pillow for my wet hair, I slipped into fresh sheets on the king-sized mattress on the floor of the loft and drifted to sleep. I tried not to miss my dog's heavy breathing in her empty bed below.

A couple of times during the night I heard Radar bark at something. She sniffed outside my window at one point, I think. Traitor, I said in my half-sleep.

CHAPTER FIVE

Hayley, barefoot and in an ivory cotton caftan, was in the kitchen nook sipping from a Bullwinkle mug when I came to the main house to invite her on my morning run. "Radar likes to get out of the yard, and besides, she's great protection when I get off the sidewalks and onto Kite Hill," I told Hayley.

"Jogging, ugh," she retorted, wrinkling her nose. "Oh, well, I need to get back in shape. Give me a sec and I'll put on something I can run in."

So that's how it was going to be this morning, like polite strangers who hadn't shared a hot tub the night before. But not quite the tension of a one-night-stand who still lingers in the morning when you just want her out of the house. We were like business associates. I could live with that. Actually, it felt pretty comfortable. At least neither of us was pretending to be madly in love or anything.

My only fear, one that maybe I should have given more weight to last night, was that our encounter could somehow hurt her recovery. Newcomers to AA aren't supposed to get into a relationship the first year. But since Hayley had been in recovery of some kind or another for more than twenty years, the rules somehow didn't seem to apply.

I wasn't sure how I felt. It was naïve to even think last night could be the start of any kind of a relationship for a Hayley Malone. But then, what was "a" Hayley Malone anyway? I had no idea how she felt either. I wasn't being fair to put her in "a" category. It must happen to celebrities a lot.

She came back wearing jeans and a yellow scoop-neck tee, with a yellow cardigan tied around her waist, her feet in sneakers. Adorable.

"Warmup first," I said, stretching sideways. Grudgingly she followed, doing about half the exercises I did.

"How's the security here?" she asked between jump-ups.

"You're looking at the best of it." I nodded toward Radar. "And you can see Kitt's got a six-foot wood fence all around the property, with thorny lemon trees lining the fence to discourage anyone climbing over."

"That explains all the lemonade and the lemons in the fridge," Hayley said.

"Got it. You need a card to get in the driveway gate, and there're deadbolts on all the doors and security steel designs on ground-floor windows. Kitt's tried magnetic contacts and those photoelectric beams and motion detectors, but she has staffers coming and going all the time, plus all her cats kept setting off false alarms, so she doesn't even turn those systems on anymore. There's a neighborhood rent-a-cop system, but they're just about worthless."

"Why?"

"They're supposed to go around at irregular times but any fool could figure out their routes. Still, I guess I'd call them instead of the LAPD if I heard something at night. For one thing, they'd probably come quicker. Their number's programmed as number one in each phone, if you ever need it. The regular police are two, fire's three, Kitt's office is four." What else did she need to know? "Oh, Kitt said she'd told the guards to come more frequently while you're here, just on general principles. She does it for all celebrities. I'd better get you a set of keys and a card."

Kitt keeps extra sets, plus her few pieces of really good jewelry, stashed in her office inside what looks like a carved wood statue of a reclining naked woman but which conceals a small compartment, cleverly hidden by the wood grain.

"Kitt told you the rest of the story about the day we found you, about the drug lab arrest?"

Hayley nodded.

"There was some talk we might have to testify

against those guys, and the police told us to be extra careful because of that, too. Plenty of bad guys out there, no doubt about it." I felt as if I were rambling. Time to get moving.

I locked up behind us and we took off through the maze of dirt and cement roads winding through the hills of Mount Washington. Depending on where you live on Mount Washington, you can have an entirely different view of L.A., and I don't mean the scenery. Mount Washington Drive from top to bottom, too much to jog in one day, reveals a cross section of L.A. class warfare.

At the very top is what used to be a luxurious resort hotel — I've never heard exactly who owns it now, though some rumors say it belongs to a cult. I could believe it. Scientology owns some of the choicest land in all of L.A., including a few blocks of prime Sunset Boulevard. Whoever owns this property, I rarely see any cars or people around, and they're not part of our Neighborhood Watch.

Several very nice homes, including Kitt's, adjoin the former hotel and sprawl down the hillside. The richest homes near the top give way to an upper-middle-class enclave clutching the hillsides, followed by solid middle- and working-class homes getting closer and closer together as the bottom looms.

"Bottom" is appropriate — the struggling home-owners and apartment-dwellers in northeast L.A. fight to keep gang graffiti off their walls, the home-less off their porches, thieves off their cars and wallets, and the understaffed, overstressed police off their case. Street people hide in alleys and live behind garages whose owners are afraid to go on parts of their own property after dark.

Wealthy whites rule the top, gays and lesbians are heavily represented among the middle-class hodgepodge along the sides, and the bottom is populated almost totally by Latin-American citizens and legal and illegal residents, plus the floating rainbow subclass of the homeless, addicts, and people in trouble with the law. Graffiti proclaims who rules each block that day. A microcosm of L.A.

The joys of living on a hill, I thought. Though I'd picked the easiest short route I could for Hayley, it was a lot harder coming home the few blocks uphill. I had to slow for Hayley to keep up. The run and the few minutes of sun did wonders for her complexion; the pale blue eyes didn't fade into a sea of gray anymore. She almost had a pink blush, including on top of her bald head.

"Whew, I'd better shower," Hayley gasped.

"Me too. See you in a few minutes." I headed for the guesthouse.

Back in her caftan, she had sandwich makings on the kitchen table when I returned to the main house. "There's not a lot of choices here. We need to go shopping. Join me for Swiss on whole wheat?"

"Sounds great. I've been thinking which are the best AA meetings, where you won't have to worry about anybody breaking anonymity."

"Forget it."

"What?"

"I don't want to go to any more AA meetings. I've been to five hundred of the damned things, plus fourteen years of therapy and five months in Betty Ford. I know everything there is to know about myself, and I'm not really an alcoholic."

Stunned, I tried to take in what I'd heard. "You

were drunk when I first saw you, before Kitt took you back to the center."

"Yeah, I'd been drinking, but that's only because that damned cherry wine showed up again. Everywhere I go, every time I try to get free, a bottle of goddamned cherry wine appears somehow." She slammed her fists on the table. "What am I saying? Of course I'm an alcoholic, and a drug addict, and I take full responsibility for ruining my own life by bad choices. It's just that I don't think I would have ever taken my first drink if someone hadn't shoved the bottle in my hand."

She glared at me. I guessed I was a stand-in for the world.

"It wouldn't bother me a bit to never drink another sip or take another hit again so long as I live, just so nobody pushes it on me. I really believe that, though I know it sounds like every other alcoholic who won't face the truth. Am I deluding myself? Am I crazy? I don't know!"

The woman was still looney. Why had Betty Ford discharged her? Or had they just given up? Take it slow, I told myself. Get her to talk it out and maybe you can make some sense of this.

"Okay, we'll just sit and talk for a while." I eased into one of the comfy padded bucket seats of the dinette set.

She smoothed her hands over her scalp absentmindedly, like the routine action of someone accustomed to playing with her hair, and jerked her hands away when she encountered only skin. She shook her head and with a wry smile, poured us both lemonade and sat.

"Whatever happened to that guy I saw with you

that day, the one you called your boyfriend and then you said he was a ghost?"

That drew her up straight in her chair. She rubbed her face in her hands. "I *was* raped. I didn't even know it until later. They did a physical exam when I arrived at the center and they told me the results when I could handle it. They passed the information on to the police, too, but everybody kept it quiet. That's the good thing about Betty Ford's."

"And the results were?"

"It was fresh semen all over me, and I don't even recall what happened. You may know more about what happened to me that day than I do."

I told her exactly what I had seen, including my description of the rapist.

"I don't have the faintest idea who that might be. Every so often in my life I get a quick glimpse of a guy who might be this same character. He's always in a T-shirt and jeans and he has a brown crew cut, just like the one you saw." She got up and looked out the kitchen window toward the pool. "Last thing I remember clearly was living in an apartment in Venice with a girlfriend I'd met my last stay at Betty Ford. We were doing really good when she started to drink again, and she started to have weird friends over. Then, one day, same as always, I got home and went to the fridge and there was a bottle of cherry wine."

She was lost in her thoughts, staring into the cloudy gray sky. I had to prompt her to continue.

"So then I drank it. It seemed like it was no use going on. Everywhere I go, this ghost follows me and sets me up with cherry wine, and I get discouraged and drink it and then it's all over. I'm out of it from that point on. Yeah, I'm an alcoholic, but I wouldn't have any trouble if that damned cherry wine didn't show up. It's easy for me not to touch alcohol otherwise."

"How long had you been on the streets when we found you last June?" I asked.

"This happened back in April or May, I'm not sure when, and I don't recall much in between. I do know I totaled my Volvo and got an insurance check for it, but I must have been robbed along the way."

"You don't seem like the Volvo type."

She laughed. "Somewhere in the back of my head, even when I'm drinking, I'm always taking care of myself. I guess I figured that if I was going to drink I was likely to drive, too, and I'd better have the safest car on the road. Anyway, I was hanging on, waiting for June one, at some point, I think I remember, and then you found me."

"What happens June one? You said something about getting your money every month?"

"It's a long story. You want to hear the story of my life, Laney? I've got nothing better to do. You have anything planned?"

I assured her I didn't, having cleared my schedule for a few days after Kitt's call had come in.

"Hey, we'll compromise and call it an AA meeting, if it makes you feel better. Start with the readings from the Big Book, I don't care. I just can't face going into some anonymous meeting and talking to a bunch of strangers who always include some nut who gets all excited when they recognize me."

"I was thinking of meetings where that wouldn't happen."

She continued as if I hadn't spoken. "Then there's always somebody trying to make themselves out to be the worst sinner in all God's creation when they're just an ordinary drunk, and there's two or three people just looking for love in all the wrong places, including AA."

I couldn't disagree.

"You need an AA meeting? Get the book, you must have one around, and put it on the table and we'll call it a meeting, okay?" She gave me that same crooked smile. I knew where a copy of the AA handbook was in Kitt's office and brought it in.

"Okay, twelve steps, blah blah. Twelve traditions, blah blah. Readings, blah. I'll start." She plopped herself back in her chair.

She started by describing her mother who was sometimes emotionally open and sometimes not, setting up a crazy-making dynamic in her needy little girl. Apparently, one way Hayley could always get her mother's attention was by singing.

"Mom tried suicide by pills a couple of times when I was growing up, and she finally succeeded right after the success of my first song. But she did one good thing before she died: she got me set up with a great accountant and insisted that I put the bulk of that first money into unbreakable trusts that gave me a decent monthly income for the rest of my life. I blew everything I earned later on, but I've never had to be flat broke."

"That must have made your life simpler," I said.

Hayley shrugged. "The bad side of that is, I never reached rock bottom financially the way a lot of drunks do. I always knew I only had to make it to the first of the next month when I could write another check. I wasn't forced to seriously face my drinking and drugs for a long, long time."

She and her mother lived with her mother's family during the Korean War while her father was away. The easiest way to get his attention when he returned was to be a sexy little flirt, "Daddy's girl."

"Songs and sex — the roots run deep." Hayley scowled.

After the war, her family moved to a small farm in the Michigan Thumb region, with blueberries being their primary crop. They had a second child, a boy, Patrick, who was blinded by an overdose of the oxygen hospitals used then to save the lives of premature infants. The tragedy particularly affected her mother. Still, Hayley called her childhood fairly average.

She was in thought. "If I can just keep the ghost away."

I didn't say anything. What was this ghost thing anyway?

"Yesterday morning I was saying good-bye to the center," she went on, "wishing I could stay forever and at the same time sick of the place. They have this beautiful reflecting pond to walk around — although they put these huge, phony plastic swans on the pond to keep away real ducks and geese so they don't shit all over the place."

I had to laugh at the picture. Even in a place dedicated to the truth, they had plastic swans.

"So I was walking around the pond and wondering what it was going to be like in the, quote, real world, glad that I had someone to take me home even though I barely knew Kitt and wasn't thrilled to be dumped on you. I felt really confident while I was still at the center, and now . . ." Her voice cracked. "That's all I can talk about today. I think I'll take a nap."

I stood and rubbed her tense shoulders.

She wasn't quite through: "Recite the Lord's Prayer, blah blah, donate a dollar, hugs, Serenity Prayer, end of meeting," she announced, and broke into tears.

I gave her the traditional AA end-of-meeting hug, with extra caring. Her thin shoulders shook, then gradually settled against me as if she were snuggling into a pillow. I kissed her lightly on her bald scalp and sent her to bed.

CHAPTER SIX

A couple of hours later Hayley knocked on the guesthouse door. "Would you mind taking me shopping for a scarf or a hat or something?" she said, rubbing her scalp.

"Sure. Having second thoughts about your hair?"

"Sunburn." Her pink scalp was definitely red now. I drove her to Glendale Galleria, my usual haunt for all-around basic shopping.

She sniffed at the scarves at the department stores and smaller shops. "They look like old lady babushkas," she said. "I'd rather go to Melrose."

Why hadn't I thought of that? Hayley was definitely not the Glendale Galleria type.

An adolescent in a Dodgers shirt was looking at Hayley's head. He'd been trailing us for a while, I realized. The "ghost" couldn't be a kid?

"Don't be obvious about it, but do you see that young man by the water fountain? He's following us."

She stole a peek, then laughed. "Hey, don't worry about him. That's the look of an autograph hound. Watch this. Bet he thinks I'm Sinead O'Connor." She deliberately smiled at the boy and let him approach her.

"You're Sigourey Weaver!" he pronounced, handing Hayley a McDonald's napkin and ballpoint. She wrinkled her nose back at me.

"Sure, Slugger," she said, signing with a flourish.

"You look a *lot* better than in that last *Alien* movie." He grinned at her and looked as if his next step might be to ask her out. Or worse.

"Hey kid, you got an older brother? Maybe your dad's free?" she asked. His face fell. "Or maybe your mom?" Hayley whispered so only I could hear and grinned over at me. "Take good care of that napkin, Slugger." She took me by the arm and walked me briskly into the next store, which happened to be a Waldenbooks.

"What did you sign?" I was curious. As we browsed I bought a consumer's buying guide to new cars. I'd been checking out the new Jeep Cherokees on the road and preparing to say good-bye to my old pickup, especially since its odometer was approaching 200,000 miles.

"Oh, I sort of ran all the letters together so you

can't tell who it is. That's my standard procedure when someone thinks I'm somebody famous but they don't know who. I must be really slipping if he thought I was Sigourey Weaver. Who am I kidding, I'm closer to her age than to Sinead's. But he gave me an idea."

From the bookstore we searched out a sports store. Hayley bought a Detroit Tigers cap and slid it around backwards on her head. The navy blue made her eyes look bluer, her skin rosier.

"Whatta ya say, Slugger?" she said, bouncing her fist off my shoulder.

In a boutique window she spotted an African-inspired hat in primary colors that the sales clerk called a kufi. I'd seen plenty of African-American lesbians wear them.

"When my 'do grows out half an inch, I'll get some mustache wax and spiff up the front and call it a buzz," she announced, admiring her new looks in the store mirror. "Right now my head looks gross — red and shiny and all cut up."

I didn't say a word. It was a credit to the shop that no one stared. Maybe they thought she was a cancer patient and they were being polite.

Next we stopped at the Safeway Superstore in Glendale for groceries. As we piled paper sacks in the back of the pickup, she asked, "Is the Pleasure Chest still around?" Vaguely I remembered the store, across from a bar called Spike that advertises itself, "Where men are men and boys are toys."

"I think so, it's been around as long as I can remember."

"Good. Would you mind driving me there?" She

gave me a dazzling smile, the kind that makes you forget what you were going to say.

I drove to Santa Monica Boulevard, three blocks east of Fairfax. The Pleasure Chest was indeed still in existence. I barely swerved in time to make the narrow driveway, set off by a yellow ocher block fence.

"Come on in," she said when I hesitated. I parked and moved the grocery sacks to inside the cab to prevent theft before entering the store. Sometimes it was a real drag to have a pickup. Jeep Cherokees danced in my head.

It was a lot different going into a sex shop these days than in the sixties, when I'd made a few furtive visits and bought a strap-on dildo to please a couple of different women in my wilder past. Or was it me that had changed?

At first glance, the Pleasure Chest looked like a stationery shop, with all sorts of greeting cards, calendars and albums on display. The color scheme was a sophisticated black and white with red accents. The first sales clerk I spotted was a woman, as were several more of the clerks on the second level, reached by a small flight of gray-carpeted stairs. The clothes on the walls could have been from any boutique — until I focused on the predominance of black leather, silver studs and chains. Froufrou petticoats danced on some displays.

"Where are your dental dams?" Hayley asked a male clerk, her voice louder than I would have liked.

He motioned to the display case behind the videos. An African-American woman with heavily-beaded cornrows came over to help her.

"Are these all you have?" Hayley asked incredulously. "Are you all sold out?"

"No, we never have had many. They don't move," the clerk said.

"Well, they're moving now. I want them all." Hayley's voice rose.

Everyone in the store stopped and turned to look at her. A woman standing next to a man at the condom display clutched his arm. I glanced through the videos.

The clerk dangled a sheet of latex in front of her own nose. "They're supposed to smell like root beer or cherry or piña colada, but it's still rubber to me," she said. "It hardly seems worth it."

Hayley stared at her, then grabbed up every one of the dental dams. "Fuck you, lady." She glared into the case. "I'll take that 'dammit' too — that's a great idea. See, Laney?" Deliberately she pulled out the leather garters and showed me how to keep the dams in place, posing for the larger audience.

I knew my face was red. Glancing around, I watched the rest of the customers go back to their own purchases.

"What kind of water-soluble lubricants do you have these days?" Hayley continued. The clerk shrugged her shoulders and brought her a dozen bottles of scents.

"Not rose," I said.

"Huh?" Hayley turned to me.

"Any scent but rose," I repeated. Rhonda's signature. Someday I'd tell her. The clerk took back one bottle.

"Okay, that's it. Oh, surgical gloves. Finger cots.

And vibrators. At least two. Which kind do you like best, Laney?"

Grudgingly I joined her at that counter and pointed to a plain variety with two speeds and various heads — the "deep muscle relaxer" was always my favorite. But we were going to have to have a long talk. As soon as we got out of here.

"Two of these, then. I think that's it. Anything else, Laney?"

A male clerk walked by and whispered "Go, girl!" in my direction. I wanted to strangle him with the nearest three-foot dildo.

Hayley paid for the purchases and followed me back to the truck. I took the groceries out of the cab and put them in the rear again. What looked like the Spike's overflow crowd hung around the parking lot. I took the narrow alley out to the side street and turned back on Santa Monica Boulevard.

"Hey, there's a 7-Eleven — I forgot to get milk for my coffee at Safeway," Hayley said. "Could you stop for a minute?"

Obligingly I turned into that driveway, trying to be inconspicuous as I caused traffic to swerve everywhere. A few years ago I would have been flashing the bird right and left at anybody who complained about my driving, but these days we all drive more politely. Giving the finger can get you shot.

She returned and put a brown paper bag inside the lavender Pleasure Chest package. I put the key in the ignition, then stopped. We needed to talk first, and we didn't have an audience here.

"What was that all about?" I asked.

"The milk?" She dug out the quart of skim milk and waved it at me, her eyes teasing.

"No, I mean what you bought back there."

"Foreplay?" Her eyes twinkled even more.

I let my exasperation show.

"Okay, no more beating around the bush," Hayley said. Her eyes changed to steel blue-gray. "Look, we can't pretend last night didn't happen, and that something else *might* happen. Last night was fine . . ." She looked in my eyes, as if to make sure I knew what she meant. "But I plan to always be careful. I took two AIDS tests at the center, one when I first went in and the other two months later, and they came out negative. But it may take longer for the antibodies to show up on tests. In almost all people they'll show up by three months, but in a few rare cases it can take as long as six months."

"I heard some news story that it was even longer."

"Oh, a couple of scientists have said it can take two to three years in extremely rare instances. You can get some expert or another to say almost anything. But the doctors I talked to said three months' wait gives virtual certainty, and that's good enough for me. We can rely on six months if you prefer. Or three years. Your call."

So we were into *the* discussion. My irritation had dissipated, replaced by that hovering fear at the back of the scalp that comes up whenever there's serious talk about AIDS. Even after I'd been on the AIDS Aid board for years.

"Anyway, before I went to Betty Ford I was living with a woman who had boyfriends on the side, and I had a few blackouts, so I can't guarantee what I did — or what was done to me," Hayley said. "And then there's the rape. So I have to get tested again in another month. Now, what about you?"

I thought back to the episode with Rhonda, and the period of worry when I found out she'd lied. "I had the test last year and it was negative. So I'm okay. But your gizmos are probably a good idea."

"Just probably?" Her eyes teased. "Nobody in the past year, you poor thing?" She put both arms around my neck and gave me a kiss that sucked the "probably" right out of me. So much for platonic business partners.

Just to tease, I guessed, she moved primly to her side of the cab for the trip home. This woman could drive me crazy.

"So why did *you* think you needed to be tested?" she asked from her window seat.

As we drove I told her all about Rhonda. She listened in silence as I rambled through the whole story.

"I thought I'd checked her out enough," I said. "I even visited the church where her husband was the Episcopal priest and saw her at his side Sunday morning."

"You never can tell these days," she acknowledged. We both pondered our own thoughts for a while.

Eventually Hayley said, "So tell me the rest of your story, and I'll tell you mine."

"Is that anything like 'you show me yours and I'll show you mine'?"

"We already did that. Now it's time to get to

know each other." Hayley grinned at me as we pulled up to Kitt's estate. Her kufi was askew on her fuzzy head.

I dug for the plastic ID card to let my truck through the wrought-iron gate.

CHAPTER SEVEN

We unpacked the groceries, put together a cold-plate supper, and then sat on the deck. She brought the Pleasure Chest bag with her, and I was conscious of its presence alongside her lawn chair as we talked.

My life story took about a hot minute. Alcoholic father, a disappearing mother, three stepmothers and other rotating relatives, despair and drinking after being purged from the Army, odd jobs till I met Anne and we bought the bar, AA, breakup last year when I felt I was being too controlled, Rhonda, and finally my new life alone.

She looked at me almost with pity. Had I sounded that depressing? Quickly I added some positives: the boards I'd been appointed to, the fund-raising and P.R. successes, the fun of making the bar succeed, the pride in making myself computer-literate, the amount of travel I'd started to do, the way I'd forged my new life.

She started with the upside too. Life on the family farm in northern Michigan — feeding the chickens and gathering eggs, giving homegrown apples to the neighbor's palominos on the way home from her one-room school — sounded like a Norman Rockwell vignette.

When Patrick needed specialized schooling, the family moved to Saginaw, a mid-sized city about a hundred miles northwest of Detroit, where her father got a job in a plastics factory that supplied John Deere tractors with dashboard dials.

The family was always in debt from Patrick's expenses, which is why they lived in a pre-dominantly black area of Saginaw, in the shabby apartment over the liquor store that finally was burned down in the 1967 racial violence.

In my mind I could hear Anne's strong feminist voice questioning why white people feel they have to give an unasked-for explanation as to why they live in an African–American neighborhood.

As Patrick grew up, he developed a friendship with Little Stevie Wonder, also born in Saginaw. Both boys liked music and shared the expertise of a specialist in music-training for the blind, who rotated throughout Michigan. Then, of course, Motown discovered Stevie, but he kept track of his friends.

Patrick insisted Stevie listen to his sister's song about the riots, and that's how Hayley came to be a rock star at age seventeen.

" 'We're All Hurting' was a more honest song than that 'Ebony and Ivory' mush he did with Paul McCartney later." Hayley sneered.

Patrick was now a director of Leader Dogs for the Blind in suburban Detroit, but he'd washed his hands of Hayley many years ago when the drugs and alcohol took over. Her father and his second wife did the same.

"Tough love, they call it," Hayley said. "And now I'm here." She got up from her lawn chair and pulled me to her and kissed me. "I need some comforting," she said, snuggling in for more kisses. When we reached the deep breathing stage, she tugged me toward the guesthouse. "Maybe I really need another nap — show me where you sleep." I noticed she grabbed for the Pleasure Chest bag as she followed me.

Inside, I showed her my loft. She took one step up on the wooden ladder and froze.

"I guess I'm afraid of heights. I'd be worrying about falling off," she said.

"So I'll bring some comforters by the sofa." I tugged linens into place.

She spread her gadgets on my small dinette table. "Take your pick."

The clerk's words rang in my ears — "Hardly

seems worth it." I looked at the display again and thought of a tray of surgical instruments. Suddenly I knew that I did not want to have sex right now.

Gently I told her. We held each other.

"Of course it's okay," she said, pulling away.

I sat down on the Herculon-upholstered sofa. The rust-and-gold plaid material itched; I wiggled to scratch my back on it.

"Hey, *I* can do that. Turn around," Hayley ordered, and she scratched my entire back and shoulders.

The problem with most people's back scratches is that they do a hit-and-run; Hayley knew to continue until every possible itch had been coaxed out and away. Sometimes I thought a good back scratch was better than sex. Almost. I told her so.

"I've got something better than a back scratch." She got to her feet and fetched a small bottle of patchouli oil. "Are you up for a massage?"

"Only a —"

"I know, I know. Take off your clothes. Hey, you don't have anything I haven't already seen." Her grin was honest.

She knew how to give a good massage, putting the oil into her palm first to warm it rather than squirting cold oil directly on the skin. All itches disappeared, perhaps forever. The backs of my calves let go of the tension I hadn't realized was there. My neck felt like a fine vase newly emerged from the potter's wheel.

"Now your front." I turned, and Hayley continued with her oils, starting with my face. I'd never had a massage that encompassed every inch of my head before. Would you believe in the sensual eye socket, the newest erotic hot spot? I wondered what my oil-soaked hair looked like in a mirror — or to her eyes. Her fingertips circled my eyes and wiped away all thoughts.

She moved down to my toes and worked up. Who would have thought toes needed to be relaxed? Her touch was enough to give me a foot fetish. I would have never thought of shins as erotic zones but under her hands they were — her long strokes up the hard bones set off arrows aimed right at the vee between my legs. As she worked her way toward my knees I wondered if they could ever hold me up again.

She detoured up the sides of my hips and found her way under my arms, also underrated as an erotic zone. I managed not to think about worn-away deodorant and simply enjoyed the kneading of flesh. She avoided all areas usually considered erogenous.

"Okay, that's it. Feel good? Need anything more anyplace?" Her cut-and-dried words and tone gave a definite ending to the massage. Lost in the luxury, I thought about saying I'd changed my mind. Coming when I felt this relaxed would be like hot fudge rolling over ice cream. I smiled to myself. Safer sex was underrated.

She kissed me lightly and got up.

So the woman had meant what she said. Good. So why was I so annoyed?

"Your turn," I said.

"Next time," she replied. She was in the bathroom starting the shower.

I waited until she was through to take mine. We

heaped the oily sheets and comforter aside and pulled out fresh ones. Would I have a wash tomorrow!

Outside it grew dark. We slept.

Around one a.m. I heard Radar running around the yard barking her fool head off. She dashed into my house through the doggie door and whined for me.

"What's the matter, Radar? You hear something out there?" Patchouli oil on the heap of soiled sheets no longer smelling sweet, I wrapped myself in a terry robe and found my slippers. "Let's check it out." I followed the running white shape as she circled the house.

"Don't bark!" I ordered in futility. The neighbors were probably far enough away that they wouldn't be bothered anyway. I could see no reason for Radar to be so frantic. She threw herself against the fence in several places. "There's nothing here," I said sharply. "Back to bed."

I tried to sleep but couldn't. What was making Radar act so crazy? Maybe rats were in the palm trees again, or a coyote was ranging the neighborhood. Raccoons and opossums sometimes found their way into the yard. Maybe some neighborhood kids were acting out, or the gangs were up this high on Mount Washington on a dare. In the morning I'd check with the families I knew.

Just briefly I thought of the drug lab guys but dismissed the thought. They were in jail, and we hadn't had to testify, and probably they had no idea who we were and that we'd been the ones to call 911, albeit for another crime in progress. Just put those worries aside, I assured myself. And there's no such thing as a ghost.

It couldn't have been an hour before Radar started to bark again, the same frantic racket that I'd tried to shut up earlier.

"Damn it," I grumbled.

"She's at it again," Hayley said.

"I'm going out right now."

"I'm going with you." Two felt better. I threw on my terry robe and gave her a nightshirt.

The sidewalk was cold and grainy on my bare feet. Strangely, the barking had stopped. All seemed quiet until I heard a moan and a small splash.

I ran to the pool. "Radar!"

She made faint, dog-paddle splashes with one paw and sank below the surface. I threw off the robe and dove in for the dog. She was limp in my arms. Hayley stripped off her nightshirt and jumped into the pool beside me.

"Radar!" I cried. I floated her to the steps and held her eighty pounds on my lap, Hayley keeping the dog in place. Having lived with a vet, I knew what to do. Putting my cheek against Radar's nose, I determined she wasn't breathing. No pulse could be found on her side or in her groin.

Heaving her up out of the water with me, I held her by her back legs and let her body swing free, to let the pool water drain out. I pulled her onto the poolside, checked to make sure her tongue was uncurled and there was nothing blocking her airpipe, and placed my mouth over her whole nose. Keeping her jaws shut, I puffed into her lungs, aiming for fifteen breaths a minute. Air in, one two, air out, one two.

"Did you ever do CPR?" I asked Hayley.

She shook her head.

Between breaths I explained how she should push down on Radar's breastbone about two inches at a time. "Think pulse rate, about a second each push," I said. We struggled for a smooth, powerful, life-giving rhythm.

It took only a few minutes until Radar let out a massive sneeze, filling my mouth with her nose secretions. I gagged and put my whole head underwater and coughed, trying to get all the mess out of my mouth, out of my sinuses. Radar shook herself loose and sneezed again, apparently trying to get my breath out of her as badly as I was trying to get her mouth juices out of me.

"You're okay!" I cried in immense relief, reaching for her to give her a big hug. To my horror, she keeled over back into the water. "Help me!" I screamed to Hayley. Together we got the dog fully out of the pool. She was still breathing, if faintly. Her left front paw seemed to hang funny. I scooped her up but stumbled after a few steps under the weight.

"I'll get a comforter — we'll make a sling," Hayley said.

"Get something for a leg splint," I yelled after her. I put my robe back on while she ran. She came back in an instant with a ruler, masking tape and the oil-scented quilted bedspread. We immobilized the paw, rolled Radar onto the spread and dragged her behind us to the garage.

"She'll be better in the back of the pickup — there's more room," Hayley said, scrambling onto the back and helping me hoist the limp body in the comforter, keeping the paw clear. It took every ounce of our combined strength. She huddled the dog close to her and held tightly to the metal sidewall. I knew she could tell I wasn't thinking straight. "You know an all-night emergency vet clinic? We'll be okay back here. Wait, go get your license and money. Maybe you should call, make sure they're open."

I had to try Anne first. She'd found Radar for me, nursed her through her puppy days, loved the dog as much as I did. She answered the phone with sleep in her voice but awakened as I poured out my story.

"I'll meet you at the clinic in a few minutes," she said as she slammed down the phone.

I had to dig under all the towels and paraphernalia for my wallet, and I grabbed some clothes for both of us, even a pink scarf for Hayley's head. I cursed the time it took to lock all doors as I left. I made up for the delay in the truck, ignoring the speed limit.

In the back of the pickup, Hayley handled even the reckless curves well, gripping both Radar and the side. In front of the Sunset Boulevard clinic, Hayley leaped out of the truck bed before I could exit the cab.

While I checked on Radar, telling her over and over that she was going to be all right, Hayley pounded on the door. Anne came out with a gurney and we got Radar to the examining room. As Anne

inserted the anal thermometer and ran the stetho-
scope over Radar's chest and back, I told her what
I'd done so far. "It came back to me — I remembered
everything you'd taught me."

"Good, good," she muttered, in response to my
actions and to her first findings. After the pre-
liminary check we moved to X-ray, where Hayley
and I helped hold Radar in place. To develop the
films, Anne shooed us out.

While waiting for Anne to finish we took turns in
the rest room putting on the clothes I'd brought. My
cutoffs hung on Hayley's hips, but the Cris
Williamson T-shirt fit snugly. Another perk from
working for Kitt — unlimited variety in women's
music T-shirts. Hayley tied the pink silk scarf so it
covered her scalp and hung like a gypsy's down one
shoulder. The color gave a soft blush to her excited
face, and she was stunningly beautiful.

Anne hadn't said a word, hadn't even seemed to
see Hayley and me, much less guess at our relationship or recognize the former singer. All for the
better. It shouldn't still matter to me, but it did.

"Radar's going to be okay," Anne finally came out
to report. She took off her blue-framed glasses to
clean them with a paper towel. Her naturally curly
salt-and-pepper hair was cut short again. She was so
strong, so professional, so . . . cute. I couldn't help
feeling a twinge of regret. Until she put her glasses
back on and with them her authoritarian posture.
"She has a slight skull fracture, where she either hit
something or got hit, and a broken leg. You said she
jumped into the pool? She could have hit her head
on the side?"

Not likely, I thought.

Hayley volunteered another theory. "She was jumping up against the fence — maybe she hit a stone or a tree branch when she came down?" From the look on her face I knew that Hayley didn't believe her own words.

"Could somebody have attacked Radar?" Anne gave me a look to imply that whatever had happened, I'd better not have put Radar in danger. I didn't answer.

For the first time Anne was able to really look at Hayley and me. I could see her face turn hard as she sized up the situation. She still didn't seem to recognize Hayley, and I hadn't given a last name when I introduced them. Her nose twitched, perhaps at the lingering scent of massage oil.

Anne seemed to wait for further explanation from me. While I debated how much to tell her, she apparently gave up on the wait and turned back to business.

"I'm going to keep Radar under observation until" — Anne checked her watch — "about three, to give her twelve hours. Come back tomorrow afternoon to get her. I'll keep a watch on her to make sure she doesn't lose consciousness or have too much pain, and I'll put a cast on that paw. Don't worry, I'll take good care of her." Anne sent us off.

I took a brochure from what seemed to be Anne's latest cause, Pets Are Wonderful Support (PAWS), which cares for the pets of people with AIDS. I'd mail them a check in the morning.

"Was I imagining things or was she cool to you?" Hayley asked outside.

"Remember the ex-lover of almost twenty years? That's Anne."

"Ah. Sorry, I hope I didn't mess things up. There's still something between you two."

"After twenty years, there's bound to be some residual feelings. Don't worry, you couldn't mess it up more than I did already. No, it's over. I don't think you want to hear all the gruesome details."

We couldn't sleep and ended up at an all-night Denny's on Sunset. Hayley didn't seem to want to talk about the present, so I asked her more about the past, particularly all those rock stars, the people Kitt had wanted to know about. "Actually, just tell me about Janis."

"So why does everybody want to know about Janis?" Hayley rolled her eyes. "Okay, okay. I'll never escape that woman."

Was she serious? Were the comparisons to Janis still a sore point?

"No, no, it's okay. I'll get over it someday." She wrinkled her nose at me to indicate she was teasing. I filed a mental note that she wasn't.

She'd made love to Janis once, when they were both at the same hotel for a rock concert. Hayley had been just nineteen, Janis nearly ten years older. She'd had a crush on Janis, while Janis didn't seem to ever quite realize who Hayley was, she recalled, sadness still showing in her eyes.

"We were really awful together." Hayley chuckled. "She was so ticklish! Janis finally came, but then she disappeared into the bathroom." Hayley shook her head at the memory. " 'I'm gonna show you a real good time,' Janis kept telling me through the bathroom door. I thought it was strange, that she closed the door when I'd just made love to her. She must have been skin-popping heroin. I'd told her I never messed with that shit."

"You never did any hard stuff?"

"Cocaine, heroin, yeah, but mostly inhaling and smoking. I never trusted crack, and I never got into shooting up. I absolutely hated needles, and besides, I checked into Synanon before anyone got to me with anything like that. My problem's just the fuckin' red wine."

After a moment Hayley recounted the rest of the story about Janis. "Finally she came back to bed and rolled toward me and passed out, just like she was in a coma. I thought she was dead and checked her breathing. It was regular and her pulse was normal."

"Was this before or after Jimi Hendrix OD'd?"

"Just before. Otherwise, I would have known to call a doctor. I didn't think it was anything serious, so I got dressed and left. But she came to for a moment and do you know what she said?"

"What?"

"She said, 'Hayley, people come to see you and me for the same reason they go to auto races and bullfights. They want to see somebody die.' "

I shivered at the words.

"That made me *really* mad. When I heard she was found dead, a few months later, I got scared. Then, when Jim Morrison died in Paris six months after that, I drove to Oakland and applied to Synanon. End of Hayley, the rock star." She fiddled with the scarf and sipped her coffee.

The caffeine could only do so much. Suddenly I

was exhausted. "Let's go home and get to sleep." I made a quick phone call to the private security force and asked them to do a thorough check around the property before we got there.

CHAPTER EIGHT

The private police were just leaving as we pulled up. "Anything in particular you wanted us to check out?" the driver of the security car asked me.

"Nope, just so you're sure nobody's around," I said. "Good night, guys, and thanks for coming by." I was sorry to see them go.

"Do you mind if I sleep in your place tonight?" Hayley asked.

"If you don't, I'll be upset." I grinned. It wasn't just for security that I wanted her near.

She still wouldn't join me in the loft, so I

dragged a double-bed futon from the main house over to mine. It was just slightly better than the floor. I had to go to Kitt's supply for more linens. We tried to sleep, conscious that Radar wasn't in her spot.

"You've got all your keys, right?" I had to check. "Lock behind you every time you go from one house to the other, even for a minute."

"Uh huh. That's what I've been doing."

I drifted into sleep — fretful, ears-open sleep.

When I awoke, I called Anne's office first thing to make sure Radar was all right. The three o'clock pickup time was still on. I poured granola for Hayley and we talked of inconsequential things, then continued Hayley's life story while we watched the clock.

"What was Synanon like?" I asked her.

"Great, for a while. I learned to sing the blues from Etta James and Little Esther Phillips when they were residents. You don't know who they were? You don't know the blues."

I acknowledged I didn't.

"Stan Kenton, Art Pepper, all kinds of musical giants passed through Synanon in the late sixties and early seventies. We all got the same treatment when we stumbled in the door — like the stupid little dope fiends we were. They'd shave your head in a second if you messed up. Guess that's what I was thinking about when I shaved mine the other day." She rubbed her stubble.

"All I remember about Synanon is something about a rattlesnake in a mailbox," I admitted.

"Yeah, it's tough, that's all people remember, when Synanon was a truly great, revolutionary

82

experiment that worked for a long, long time. Fifteen or twenty years before it went sour."

"What happened?"

"Oh, the guy who founded it, Chuck Dederich, was a true genius, but he needed somebody to keep his ego in check. He found a woman named Betty who was perfect for him, and she was the real reason Synanon succeeded so long."

I wasn't really interested, but the hands of the clock had barely hit one, and she seemed to want to talk about this part of her life.

"We played something called the Synanon Game — it wasn't really therapy, but it was a way for the group to get a newcomer to shape up," Hayley said. "We did it by dumping our anger, pouring on the group pressure, making fun of behavior, whatever it took. It could be devastating."

"No, thanks," I said. "People need self-esteem, not to be yelled at."

"Yeah, well, I think addicts need both. Betty would come into a Game where somebody had been smashed into the ground and she'd start Betty's Game — telling the person all the good things about themselves. That was more devastating, more ego-shattering, than anything on earth, and you'd shape up in a second. At least I did. I owe Synanon my life."

"So what happened?"

"To me or to Synanon?"

"Both."

"Well, Betty Dederich died a long and drawn-out death from cancer and Chuck Dederich started drinking again and the place went to hell from the top."

"And you?" I prompted her when she seemed to have drifted off.

"As for me, my ghost somehow got a bottle of sweet cherry wine delivered to me after I'd done a benefit concert for Synanon. They threw me in the Game and tried to get me to confess. I guess I finally did. It sounded stupid to say that wine keeps showing up around me without my knowing how it got there."

"Is that how cherry wine got to be your trademark? I just thought you copied Janis with her Southern Comfort."

"Everybody did. Honest, every time I performed for the public, starting with my first solo concert without Stevie Wonder, a bottle of cherry wine would be delivered to me backstage before I went on. Sometimes there'd be a note telling me a sip would help me relax and sing better. So I'd take a drink, and then I'd bring it on stage with me. I was just a teenager, but the cops never busted me for it. When I didn't know what to say between songs, I'd take a swig. The audience loved it."

She rushed to the sink and gave a dry heave. She hung over the sink for a long moment, then went to the fridge and got us both Diet Pepsis. I wanted to offer her something, Advil or Pepto-Bismol, but a drug, even an over-the-counter kind, hardly seemed appropriate.

The clock seemed stalled. I took a break and walked around the perimeter of the estate again but found nothing. The security guard patrol car drove by and I chatted with them a while, informing them of the attack on Radar. They looked around some more themselves. Nothing.

Hayley was still sitting in the kitchen when I returned. I checked phone messages, changed the kitty litter, and made a few calls.

"Are you up for a fruit salad?" I asked. She nodded and I made two plates.

To break the silence, I asked what she did after Synanon. Devouring an orange slice, she snapped out of her funk and chattered away.

"Oh, I hung around Shell House, a women's commune in Venice, for a few years, stoned and drunk again. I tried to make a comeback with a women's band but it didn't work out."

I remembered. That was her disastrous appearance on Johnny Carson.

"One of the women — her name was Donna — started playing these really soothing, hypnotic tapes by Bhagwan Shree Rajneesh all day long, and she wore only the colors of the sunrise. She looked so pretty in yellows and reds, so I gave away most of my clothes too. The tapes drove everybody else nuts, but he made so much sense, and he was so full of love." She pulled out the words *so* and *love* to a drawl. "When Donna packed her bags and flew to Poona, India, to be with him, I tagged along. I didn't have anything better to do with my life. Donna said Bhagwan would take care of us, and those were the magic words."

"When was this?"

"Around nineteen eighty. We both ended up at his community in Antelope, Oregon in 'eighty-one. I'm afraid my monthly checks helped pay for his 'ninety-three Rolls Royces for a couple of years."

"Didn't they call him the swami of sex or something?"

She chuckled. "Yeah. Quite a contrast from Synanon, where you had to get approval from your tribe leader to have sex with somebody, always in the context of an approved relationship, and then you had to make an appointment for one of the few rooms with any privacy. I learned about rubber gloves and dental dams from Bhagwan."

"Then he got arrested."

"Yeah, for overstaying his visa. I moved to a women's commune in Eugene. To show you how stupid I was, I did an instant replay and followed some woman who believed in the Harmonic Convergence."

"What the hell was that?"

"Some art history teacher from Boulder wrote a book — wait, I remember the title. It was *The Mayan Factor: Paths Beyond Technology*, saying that Mars, Venus and Mercury would line up with the new moon on August sixteenth, nineteen eighty-seven, which would move the earth from one age to another. We got a hundred and forty-four thousand people to Mount Shasta to hum for two days."

I had to giggle.

"That's right, we *hummed* for two days" — she rolled her eyes — "to bring in a new age of peace and harmony. Lots of people gathered at so-called sacred sites all over the world — the Great Pyramids of Egypt, Ayers Rock in Australia."

"What happened?"

"Absolutely nothing." She had to laugh along with me. "I got so depressed that I went on a binge and ended up at Betty Ford for the first time."

"Why didn't it take?" My question made her happy chattering come to a halt.

She paused. "It did — till the next time I got the wine." Hayley scowled. "Isn't it time for us to pick up Radar?" It was.

At Anne's, Radar tried to run out to greet us, looking down in annoyance at the plaster on her paw. She was wobbly on her feet when she tried to jump up and lick our faces.

"She's fine, just groggy from the medications. Try to keep her rested for the next few days. You can take her home now," Anne said, staring openly at Hayley's scalp. She gave me a form sheet of instructions and a two weeks' regimen of antibiotics. "I've included a sedative for the next few days to help you keep her off her feet as much as possible. Don't stop until all the pills are gone," she ordered.

Radar insisted on sitting in the front seat and tugged at Hayley to make sure she squeezed in too, not the most comfortable ride. As we drove away, Radar slurped both our faces.

Back home, Radar quickly learned to race around the yard on three legs, though she was wobbly from the medications. Before calling her in, I let her sniff once more at the places on the fence where she had jumped against it the previous night. She climbed awkwardly through her doggie door and immediately reemerged, a definite canine smile on her face.

"If you're happy, I'm happy," I told her, giving her another hug.

"I'll go get lemonade. We can sit outside for a while," Hayley said. I kept hugging Radar, burying my face in her rough white fur. What a great dog! She lay on her bed and went to sleep, clearly a deep sleep.

From inside the big house Hayley screamed.

Radar raised her head, tried to get up, then plopped back on her bed. Her eyes rolled in powerlessness. She tried again.

"Stay!" I ordered her as I raced to the back door.

The refrigerator door swung open on its hinges. Hayley stood at the sink, her face buried in her hands. The refrigerator was more full than usual, thanks to our shopping trip. And then I saw the bottle on the top shelf. A half-empty bottle of Manischewitz sweet cherry wine.

Between shrieks, Hayley cried out to me, "It's my ghost! My ghost!"

She shook so hard I could barely hold her. "Stop it, Hayley. You've got to tell me what happened." She kept sobbing, flailing her arms at me. I released her. She just stood there, wailing.

For one helpless moment I could see why the traditional way to stop hysteria was a slap across the face. I wouldn't do that to her, but what else could I do? I waited. She finally turned to me and collapsed on my shoulder.

The crying turned to deep moaning. Gently I walked her over to the refrigerator, supporting her weight with one arm, and with my free arm I grabbed the bottle and maneuvered us to the sink. The wine made a glugging sound as I poured it out and placed the bottle in the trash compactor. She wouldn't drink from this bottle. Or had she already? I smelled no alcohol on her breath.

As if dancing with a child, I half-carried Hayley to the breakfast nook and sat her down. I cracked loose an ice cube tray and rolled half of the cubes in a terry dish towel for her forehead, the other half going into a glass of water that I tried to place in her hand. She shook too badly. With both hands I carefully placed the glass on the table. I waited.

When the crying stopped she sipped at the water, her eyes glazed and distant.

"Hayley?"

She didn't respond.

I remembered that she had gone into the 7-Eleven near the Pleasure Chest the day before. Did 7-Eleven carry a kosher dessert wine among its Buds and Millers and Seagram wine coolers?

"Tell me what happened, Hayley."

She wouldn't look at me, staring out the window, looking at something far, far beyond the pool. I waited.

Suddenly she made a dash down the hall for the nearest bathroom. Had she taken the wine and it made her sick? Or was she having the dry heaves again? No, she didn't spend more than a second in that bathroom before she took off for the one in the guest suite. More screams. I followed her and found her leaning over the toilet, staring into the water with a blank expression.

"Are you sick? Do you need to throw up?"

She just stood there. As she weaved toward the bathtub I caught her and lowered her body to the tile floor. Something floating in the toilet caught my eye. A doll. In pieces. An eight-inch, rounded pink plastic baby doll, the legs and arms bobbing along the edges of the water, the submerged, smirking Kewpie-doll head blocking the hole in the bottom rear of the bowl. The water had a tinge of pink, as if colored with a few drops of blood. I sniffed alcohol. Was that what had happened to the rest of the wine?

Hayley moaned. I stood up, feeling helpless.

"What happened, Hayley?"

No answer. Finally I took her by the shoulders and raised her to her feet. She was a dead weight in my arms. I tried to maneuver her back toward a chair in the breakfast nook. It was no use. I carried her down the hall and around the corner to the bed in her room and laid her on the tightly tucked Madras plaid spread. Is this what catatonia looked like? Was she having a psychotic episode, whatever *that* looked like? Should I call an ambulance?

I bent over to examine her more closely. She was breathing okay. Her eyes were open, unfocused. It couldn't hurt to wait a few minutes and try to bring her out of it. I lay down beside her and stroked her forehead. She buried her face in my shoulder — a good sign, she was *there*. After a while she rolled over on her back and stared at the ceiling.

"Tell me what happened, Hayley." I said again, then repeated the order with more force.

Finally she spoke. "I'll tell you. Give me a minute. Could I have some more ice water?" I got up and brought her the glass. She raised herself on one arm to take the drink, which she gulped down and handed to me for a refill. When I returned, she whispered, "I've never told a soul what I'm about to tell you. Don't tell anybody, please. They'll think I'm crazy."

Sitting down on the edge of the bed so that I could hold her if she wanted, I promised. My head reeled with all the worst possible scenarios. What had I gotten myself into?

I wanted to look her in the face. Gingerly I reached for her and she pushed my arm away. She lay back, rigid in the bed, examining the ceiling again.

"There's a reason for my ghost," she whispered.

CHAPTER NINE

Hayley told her story in flat tones at first, showing no emotion. "It wasn't quite as happy in Cadatunk as I made it sound the last time we talked. I never got along with my classmates at the one-room schoolhouse because I was from the city, and Mom kept drifting in and out so I never knew what to expect." She paused for a few moments, as if to collect herself. "One day, I think it was late summer just before we went back to school, Mom was acting more strange than usual. I remember that she'd been worried about what to do with Patrick's schooling, and the blueberry stand was in trouble. Up until then our family had been pretending nothing was wrong — if we ignored the problem it would go away."

In AA the usual analogy is the elephant in the living room that no one talks about.

"Patrick must have been outside in the yard Dad had fenced in for him so he wouldn't stray too far. We raised chickens and rabbits for food, and taking care of them was Patrick's job. Dad was off at the blueberry fields."

Now she was really quiet. I moved closer to her so that I could hear her soft words.

"Mom was in the bedroom. She had the door closed, which was unusual, and she was making a lot of strange noises. I thought she was sick and I opened the door a crack to spy on her. She was lying on their bed. I can still see the white chenille bedspread, so worn it was almost transparent." Hayley stopped. I held my breath and willed her to go on. "Mom opened her eyes and spotted me. At first she ordered me to go away, but then she doubled over in the bed like she'd been kicked in the stomach and she groaned really loud. She asked me to go find the pail we use to wash the floors, and to rinse it out good and then bring it in to her. I did. 'Go find your brother and keep him out of the house,' she said next." Rubbing the back of her head hard for a minute, Hayley's face showed a flash of her usual spirit. "He was already out of the house so I didn't see any need to follow her orders. I kept opening the door a crack and she kept making me close it. She finally yelled at me to keep it shut and go away. I didn't, of course — I kept my ear right up to the door."

I pictured a little girl listening to her mother's moans and imagining the worst, when she probably had no idea what "the worst" possibly could be.

"I heard sounds like she was going to the bathroom in loud gushes and spurts that echoed in the metal pail. Then she yelled out for me to bring her all the towels I could find. I was glad for the excuse to get inside." Her pale eyes darted as if involuntarily repeating the moment. "She was sitting on the pail like a toilet, and she was crying and dripping with sweat. The room smelled funny, like diarrhea, but some other heavy smell, too." Lowering her voice slightly, she imitated her mother: " 'Just give me the towels and go back outside and take care of Patrick,' she told me. Reluctantly I closed the door on her and kept my ear pressed to the wood. She kept making crying sounds, and finally she was quiet."

Hayley was quiet for a few moments as well. It seemed to hurt her to talk again.

"Very slowly I opened the door. She was in the bed and there was red all over the white chenille. I knew then that I'd been smelling blood. I thought she was dead. But she lifted her head and told me she had a big favor to ask." Hayley's voice lowered again as she imitated her mother. " 'Pick up the phone and keep hitting the buttons that the receiver rests on, until the operator comes on the line,' Mom told me. 'Ask her to call Doctor Weisskopf in Bad Axe.' I turned to go and she called me back." The lower voice again: " 'Have her call a Catholic priest too. Tell her I'm having a miscarriage. Do you understand?' I nodded, and she made me repeat what she wanted."

Poor little girl, I murmured to myself. I wanted to comfort her but I didn't want to interrupt the flow of her memories.

"The operator tried to reassure me that everything would be all right, but I could sense that she was dying to find out more herself and spread the gossip. I told Mom I'd made the call, and she asked me to take the pail into the bathroom. She was gagging at the smells too." The ersatz voice wavered this time. " 'Whatever you do, don't look in it,' she said, so of course I did. It looked like diarrhea and blood — bright red blood and dark wine blood — but there was something else, something that looked like a tiny doll's arm."

I shuddered. Hayley described how she flushed the pail's contents down the toilet and rinsed it out and took the pail outside and hurled it into the drainage ditch because she couldn't stand to have it in the house.

"Mom was sleeping — I went up to her chest to check her breathing. I brought all the messy towels to the washtub in the utility room and filled the tub with water to let them soak. I went outside to check on Patrick and he was shucking corn for the chickens. The doctor arrived in about half an hour, and I took him to mom's room. He shut me out. In a few minutes he asked to see the pail. 'It's in the ditch,' I said. 'I emptied it.' " She shifted position and drank more water. "I suddenly sensed I had done something very wrong, but I didn't know what. 'It can't be helped,' he said finally, and used our phone to call an ambulance. He said to have my father get to the hospital as soon as possible. 'She's still bleeding — never mind, just tell your father to get to the hospital.' He made me repeat the message, just like my mother did."

Hayley's face still showed annoyance, thirty-five years later. "Just then the priest drove up. I'd seen him a few times before, when Mom got someone to drive us to church in Bad Axe. He looked down his nose at our little house, gave me this sweet little pursed-up smile, and let me lead him to the bedroom. I didn't trust him, so I waited right outside. He came out in a few minutes and asked for the pail too. I told him what I'd done. From the look on his face, this time I really knew I'd done something terrible."

I was seething at this unknown priest. But Hayley went on with her story. " 'You've condemned that baby to limbo,' he said. He'd used the same booming, foreboding voice when he gave his sermons. I thought, baby? What baby? That arm was a baby? I was as horrified as it is possible to be. When I asked him how I'd done that, he said, 'I am unable to baptize the baby, and so it will never be able to see the face of God and fulfill its purpose in Heaven. That poor baby's soul will drift in limbo forever. May God have mercy on your soul.' He made the sign of the cross at me like I was a vampire or something, and he left."

"What did you do?" I asked.

"What could I do? I'd just damned a baby by flushing it down the toilet. I got out a book my grandfather had given me, a kind of Catholic dictionary for young people, and I looked up *limbo*, then *baptism.* Limbo sounded just as empty and cruel as the priest had said."

I tried to remember from my own *Baltimore Catechism* instruction what limbo was.

"But the book said that in extreme circumstances, anybody could do a baptism, not just a priest," Hayley continued. "All you had to do was to pour water on the baby's forehead while you said the words, 'I baptize thee in the name of the Father, Son and Holy Ghost.' I went to the bathroom and thought for a minute. Maybe the baby was still alive somehow. I didn't want to take any chances, just in case there was some way I could redeem my soul from this horrible sin. So I flushed the toilet so that there would be water flowing over the baby's forehead and I said the words. It didn't really make me feel any better, but it was all that I *could* do." She was sitting up straight now. "Stupid priest. All my life I've pictured this poor baby's soul, floating around somewhere, unable to go to heaven, following me because it was my fault."

"You know better now," I said gently. "It wasn't your fault. Your mother had a miscarriage, and that wasn't your fault either. Even the church doesn't talk about limbo anymore." I rubbed her back and shoulders.

"I *know* that," she said, slumping. "And yet . . ."

"And what?"

"I don't know how else to explain why baby dolls appear in my toilets and cherry wine arrives at my concerts. The baby today would be an adult, somewhere around the age of the ghost I sometimes see. I think I'm being *haunted.*"

She looked up at me with woeful eyes like a

basset hound's that would have made me laugh, except for the fact that I too had seen the baby doll parts and the wine. For a second I almost doubted myself. But then, I'd touched the wine bottle, I'd put it in the trash.

Carefully I let myself stand up and walk back to the bathroom to get the doll out of the toilet. I needed to look at it again, to assure myself it was real. Maybe it would yield some clue.

There was nothing there. The water in the toilet bowl was still tinged pink and the faint smell of alcohol lingered, but there was no plastic Kewpie doll.

CHAPTER TEN

I sank down onto the edge of the tub. Someone
had to have been in the house, even while we'd
talked — maybe still there! Somebody who'd tried to
kill Radar last night and who'd left the wine and
the doll had come back to take the doll, all the
while Hayley and I were in the other room.

Instantly I felt vulnerable and isolated, as if I
were a treed raccoon with baying hounds pointing
me out to a circle of hidden shotguns somewhere in
the dark, all aimed at my heart.

I sat there, paralyzed in fear, until I couldn't

stand it any longer. I jumped up and rushed through the house, looking for anybody, traces of any third presence, and found nothing. What if I had? I hate guns, had disliked them even when I was in Army basic training, but I felt naked, chasing an unseen criminal unarmed. I ran in spurts and dashes as if dodging bullets that hadn't shot down the gun barrel yet.

Over at the guesthouse Radar slept, her breaths heavy and labored. Wishing she could accompany me, I picked up a long wood-handled stainless steel fork from the outdoor gas barbecue next to the hot tub and brandished it fiercely as I circled the property. Nothing. Surveying the tool, I felt sheepish — what was I going to do to the guy, flip him like a porkchop? I put the fork back.

Inside the house, I checked on Hayley, who seemed to be asleep, or perhaps it was a faint. She seemed to pass out easily; maybe it was another line of defense when drinking wasn't available.

The Manischewitz bottle was still in the disposal. I took it out and put it on the counter, in case something could be determined from it. By handling it, I'd already destroyed any fingerprints. *If* this "ghost" left prints. On second thought, I hid the bottle under the sink in a paper bag, behind boxes of Brillo pads and Jet Dry. No sense rattling Hayley again.

I dialed the security company, and a silver and blue fleet car arrived at the gate within moments.

How should I explain what had just happened? Certainly I didn't want Hayley dragged into this, or any talk about ghosts. What did I want from this visit? Not a thorough investigation, because that meant publicity. I felt protective toward the huddled woman in the bedroom.

Calling the security company had seemed the right thing to do at the time, but now what? Maybe I should just have them drive by more frequently. Okay, Laney, I told myself, you're in charge. I squared my shoulders and tried to think as I talked.

"Hi, fellas, thanks for responding so promptly."

"That's what you pay us for." The taller of the two men smiled. He was too heavy to be on a regular police force, though from the way his shoulders, arms and thighs bulged against the navy uniform, I wouldn't have wanted to try to escape him. The LAPD probably wouldn't have allowed his stringy blond ponytail either. "Nothing urgent, I take it?" He checked a blue folder, then looked up at me. "You're Laney Samms. Is Kitt Meyers here?"

"She's out of town. I called you because I suspect that someone was inside the house, although there's nothing concrete I can point to." Nothing I wanted to tell them. Maybe it was time to remind them about the drug lab people. They became more alert as I told them how the LAPD had warned us about possible revenge from that event. "I've already checked around the house, but maybe you could look around the property a little more closely, see if you find any footprints or signs of trespassing," I told them. "I'd like you to check the other side of the fence around the property for any indication that it's been scaled."

"Can do, Ms. Samms." He looked again in his folder. "Where's the German shepherd?"

"Sick — she won't come at you."

He walked to the closest part of the fence and

examined the ground and the walnut-stained wood. His silent partner followed.

"Watch the lemon tree thorns," I called to their backs. I recalled that Kitt kept a cedar chip mulch around the base of the trees — they wouldn't find footprints.

Back inside, Hayley was still passive.

"I've got the rent-a-cops checking for signs of anybody climbing the fence or anything else they can find," I told her.

"Ghosts don't need to climb fences," she said in her flat, toneless voice.

"This isn't a ghost. This doesn't have anything to do with the drug lab people either. Somebody is stalking *you*. Probably a fan."

"How could that be? What fan would know about the miscarriage? What fan would just leave dolls in the toilet and never show himself, for twenty-some years! What payoff is there in that?"

"I don't know. It just has to be somebody, not a ghost. You're not crazy, Hayley."

"If I'm not, then there's such a thing as ghosts."

"We'll talk about it after I find out if the security guards found anything. Stay here, no sense getting you involved."

"I'm thankful I got *you* involved," she called as I left.

The security force found nothing inside or surrounding the property. They promised to check even more frequently, at a higher cost per month, which I authorized. Kitt would approve.

When I called, none of the neighbors reported seeing anything unusual lately. Oh, one family which has a private dirt road feeding off of Mount

Washington Drive to the rear of their house, to save themselves seventy-three steps up from the paved street, awoke one morning to find a couple hundred empty beer bottles lining the private road. They'd taken it as a gang making its presence felt, letting the rich folks know who really controlled the world around them. But the same thing had happened to that house before — maybe a bunch of guys just liked to enjoy the panoramic view from the top of Mount Washington as they partied — and I didn't think it had anything to do with Hayley. All the neighbors promised to keep a look out for anyone crawling our fence or anything else suspicious. Of course I didn't mention our famous guest. Nobody answered the bell at the gate of the former hotel.

I called information for the number of the 7-Eleven on Santa Monica Boulevard. "Do you carry Manischewitz cherry wine?" I asked the manager.

He sounded about seventeen and his voice conveyed the distinct impression that I bored him. Probably everything did. "No, lady, though you can check with our store in the Fairfax district." Wilshire–Fairfax hosts a concentration of elderly Jewish residents. "I seriously doubt it. We all carry pretty much the same thing. Want their number?"

"No, thanks." So Hayley couldn't have bought the wine as I'd first suspected — then hoped. The unmistakable conclusion was still looming.

I'd done all I could. I called Kitt's business office in West Hollywood and got one of her aides to track her down on the cruise ship.

"What's up," Kitt said when she came to the phone, the sound of crashing sea waves and laughing vacationers behind her. I told her all that had happened, and what I had done so far. She was speechless, though the background party-goers weren't.

"You got me into this. Do you know something else you're keeping from me?" I demanded.

"Honest, this comes as a complete shock. Do you want me to come home? I can probably get off this ship somehow, they must have a helicopter or something. Though I still have a lot of work to do here." I could tell she'd rather not leave.

I debated insisting she return. What else could she do that I hadn't done?

"Look, you're absolutely sure you don't know anything that might give me some answers to what's going on?" I asked again. She assured me she didn't. Something in her voice made me wait for amplification.

The silence did her in. "Well, I did know about cherry wine showing up in her life from her days at Shell House. A bottle arrived the day she was to do Carson."

"Was it Manischewitz?"

"No, some winery in Michigan. Saint something, I think, but I can't be sure after this long. I remember being surprised that there was a winery in Michigan and Hayley said that there were quite a few, that a lot of the cherry wine bottles she got came from Michigan. I don't know if that's a clue or not, but go with it."

"What do you mean?" I asked.

"Look, Laney, I didn't hire you for your looks. I was really impressed with the way you figured out the Rhonda thing for the police, even if you were acting like a dork over her for a while. I guess I had it in the back of my mind that you'd be a good person to have around if any of my people got into trouble. And here it is."

I stared into the phone.

"I have complete trust that you'll do the best thing possible, no matter what happens," Kitt continued. "If you make a mistake, it will probably be the same mistake I'd make. Just keep your wits about you and keep looking over your shoulder." She paused. "You're right that this isn't the drug people. It has to be a stalker, no matter what Hayley says. You've been wise to rely on the security guards so far. Hayley seems awfully fragile to me, and the publicity could hurt her badly. But the moment you think you need the LAPD, call them in. Your safety is more important than an image. You both might want to move out of the place for a bit."

I thought about it. "Whatever's going on, I'd rather face it on home turf than having it lurk out there somewhere."

"Good point. So maybe you want someone else there to stay with you both. Call some friends, or hey, hire a bodyguard. There's a company listed in the *Gay Community Yellow Pages* I've used before. It's up to you."

I thanked her for the vote of confidence and hung up. I wondered who to call and couldn't decide on anyone. Finally I called my old friend Max and left a message on her machine. An unflappable, tough old dyke if ever there was one, she also had a monster attack dog that could stand in for Radar. I called the bodyguard service and waited for return calls.

Knowing somebody had sneaked into the house

and was probably watching us somehow, I felt tingly and nervous for the rest of the day. I was extra-careful to lock all the deadbolts, something I don't always remember to do. It feels like a prison to me, locking doors behind you everywhere you go, but this time I welcomed the grating sound of the deadbolts grinding into place.

Between naps, Hayley walked around like a zombie, unwilling to talk about anything. Radar seemed better after devouring kibble soaked in warm Campbell's chicken gumbo — left over from the "meal" of canned soup and salad I'd thrown together — and lay at my side while I kept watch. For what, I didn't know. I did know it wasn't a ghost. From all that Hayley had told me, I tried to figure out who could be stalking her. Since she'd said the telephone operator had probably told everybody in town about the miscarriage and the priest, that meant almost anyone could be involved. But how many would know about the toilet bowl scene?

I made some calls to track down the numbers on the wine bottle, but all I found out was when and where it had been bottled; it could have been purchased at hundreds of outlets in Southern California.

Evening came, and I left on every light in the house. The big house had too many rooms. I made the rounds constantly, checking all windows and doors, doing the routine chores like changing the litter boxes and checking the answering machine while constantly glancing back over my shoulder.

The bed linens needed washing, due to the

The bed linens needed washing, due to the fragrant — now smelly — oils of the previous night that seemed an eternity ago, so I did three loads of laundry. Then I dug out Hayley's dirty clothes for a fourth load.

Everything on television seemed inane. All through the house floors creaked, windows rattled, kittens rustled newspapers, the refrigerator clunked on and off, an air conditioner roared. I convinced Hayley to move to my house for the night.

She still wouldn't sleep in the loft and I didn't want to leave her alone, so we spread the fresh comforters on the futon and dozed sporadically, her head on my shoulder. At our feet, Radar snored, twitching from pharmaceutically amplified doggie dreams.

My message to Max had said to call whenever she got in, no matter the time, and the clock across the room read 2:47 a.m. when the phone rang. I was trying to explain the problem when I realized that she was with someone.

To hell with it. We'd made it this far through the night. "Call me in the morning when you're alone," I said and hung up.

I huddled next to Hayley again and tried to sleep while keeping both ears open for any sounds. I may have slept a few moments. No dreams, just suffocating nervous exhaustion that kept a blanket over the fear.

Pink-tinged sunlight streamed in, awaking us both. So I'd finally dozed a little. "It's morning. Eight-thirty," I said, checking my watch between yawns. The red-lit digits across the room confirmed the time. My neck was stiff from sleeping upright. From being on alert while trying to sleep upright.

"Did Radar bark at all during the night?" Hayley asked.

"She never moved a muscle. So whoever it was didn't come back. Or she was too out of it to know." Mentally I dared Hayley to use the word *ghost*. She didn't, hitting the bathroom instead.

The phone rang. A highly recommended female bodyguard would be over within the hour, hired to work each day eight a.m. to four p.m. for the duration. They'd keep working on finding somebody for the afternoon and night shifts. This one would be armed. Did I say I hate guns? I lied.

Max called from her job. I explained the situation.

"No problem. My friend's in trouble, I'll be there. Not just tonight, right? I should bring some clothes, right? This is going to go on a while?"

"I haven't the foggiest. I've got a bodyguard coming in eight to four now, and the security patrol is watching the property more closely. I'll feel a lot better if there's somebody else in the house at night till we get the rest of the shifts covered, that's all."

"You got it, Laney. Say, I still don't understand what's going on . . ."

"I'll tell you tonight. You get off, when?"

"Be there by six-thirty. I'll stop for El Pollo Loco, all right?"

"Great. Plenty of tortillas and salsa."

As I hung up, a white Corolla pulled into the driveway, with a woman in uniform at the wheel. I went outside to let her in and show her around the grounds, giving an overview of the situation as we walked. The woman, Val Estrada, oozed self-confidence and strength and made me feel better already. Hayley came out of her room in a fog and looked bleary-eyed during the introduction. Val glanced at me sharply.

"She's been through a lot," I found myself defending Hayley. "Look, Hayley, I want to tell Val the whole story, even the stuff you told me yesterday, in case she can see some sort of pattern or get some clue."

"It sounds like you're in deep trouble, and I need to know everything," Val said, trying to elicit some kind of response from the shadowlike gamin.

Hayley threw up her hands. "It doesn't matter. Tell her everything. Nothing's going to stop him. Nothing can stop a ghost." She retreated to her room.

The bodyguard grew even more alert. "Does she need medical attention? Is she seeing a therapist?"

"Let me tell you everything first. She's okay for now," I said, directing Val to beach chairs outside where we could keep watch over the grounds.

Val looked like she'd been living all of her thirty years at Gold's Gym. "I took the San Diego title in the nineteen eighty-nine Ms. California body-building competition," she boasted. She'd been hired to protect several female entertainers before and sometimes worked undercover, sometimes in the blue and navy uniform she wore now.

To give her the whole picture, I went through every detail I could remember for her, including all of Hayley's life story.

She retraced the work of the security guards and

found some broken branches on several of the lemon trees that they had missed. "Here's where he came over the wall. And here. He's no ghost. Shall we show this to Hayley?"

"I think she's sleeping." Suddenly I was exhausted. A pro was in charge. "I need to go to sleep. Desperately. Can you handle everything? I'll be in the guesthouse." And with that I headed for my bed.

CHAPTER ELEVEN

Val woke me up before she went off duty. "The stalker didn't turn up," she assured me. "And I didn't find anything else. Your friend isn't due until six-thirty. Wish I could stay but I've got a night gig."

Everything seemed unreal, nonthreatening at the moment. Normal.

Except for the wine in the fridge and the doll in the toilet and a cast on Radar's foot and broken tree branches by the fence.

"Okay, we'll sit tight. Thanks for being here, Val. See you tomorrow morning."

I dragged Hayley out of her room and into the deck chairs for the time we'd be alone. It felt better to be able to see all around.

Max finally arrived in her silver Suzuki Samurai. She'd dyed her hair a mahogany brown, even harsher on her overly tanned complexion than the ash blond she'd had before. All the years of heavy smoking, drinking and tanning had long ago turned her skin to wrinkled leather. No, fine-grained wood.

A brown and black Rottweiler leaned out the plastic window, bared its fangs and growled at me.

"Easy, Frank," she rubbed its head.

"Frank?" I asked.

"After an asshole boss I once had. I loved dragging him to obedience school and making Frank follow my every command. Hey, this is Hayley Malone? Pleased to meet'cha."

"Can I fill Max in on everything?" I asked Hayley after we'd parked the cars and gone inside. I was thinking of the pool for later, though maybe that would leave us too vulnerable to someone breaking into the grounds.

"What the hell? Who cares? It's my life, welcome to it, do what you want with it," she shouted, heading for her room. Max and I pulled up lawn chairs and prepared to eat chicken when Frank sniffed the air and took off running. Max and I looked at each other.

"Don't stop him, he may be onto something," I yelled, throwing my plate on my chair and running after the massive dog.

He was onto something all right — he was heading for Radar's doggie door where she slept unsuspectingly in her comforter just inside the guesthouse.

"Stop him," I shrieked. Sickly Radar would be no match for Frank.

"Stop! Down! Stay!" Max called. To my relief the husky black and tan dog obeyed each command.

"Will he obey me?"

"Once he gets the idea that I want him to, he will. Frank, come here." And we went back to the lawn chairs where I wiped salsa off the webbed seat and proceeded to tell her the whole story as Frank sniffed the deck area. Max was as dumbfounded as I was at the three days' events.

"Hey, what are friends for? I'll stick with you till the other bodyguards sign on," Max said, chomping on a drumstick as if it were the stalker. Her cigarette dangled from the edge of her paper plate. I made Hayley a plate and brought it to her room. She was sleeping, so I left it on her bedside table with a glass of lemonade.

"Now what?" Max asked. A production control manager at a factory in Artesia that makes CD players, she was in her nerdy work clothes: a white shirt complete with pocket protector and plastic photo ID card, brown and yellow pin-striped tie, brown gabardine pants and loafers. I knew the secret of the tight white undershirt to bind the breasts and complete the look. And she was still smoking and letting ashes fall where they may, usually on my foot. Gotta love her.

"Now we keep our wits about us and watch for

any signs of anything out of the ordinary," I said. "Excuse me while I make some calls," I said, and brought a cordless phone outside.

September had slipped in the day before, and the sun set earlier than I expected.

First I called my AA sponsor, gave her sketchy information about the crisis I faced without mentioning Hayley by name, and assured her I was having no temptation to drink. "Just the opposite — seeing this celebrity go through this shit reminds me of the mess alcohol made of my life before," I told her. "Oh, hell, I trust you, it's Hayley Malone."

The name didn't register with my sponsor. Her name is Mara Wilgrein, a Latvian-born grandmother who became a lesbian — with a vengeance — once all her children were out the door. She wears her still-dark hair in one long braid to her waist and dabbles with WICCA witchcraft, when she's not giving out sage advice based on seventy years of intensive living. She left behind her alcoholism as well as her husband when she came out.

I told her the whole story, starting with the drug lab arrest, and going into the danger we now felt.

Mara was fully supportive, though she urged me to try to find time for a regular weekly meeting, to ensure that I had a strong foundation during this crisis period. I told her I'd try but could make no promises. She appreciated the story of how Hayley had made an impromptu meeting of one of our talks, adding, "Sure, I'd call that a meeting. Wasn't it Bill W. who said, 'Wherever two or more of you are gathered in my name, there am I'? Oh, that was Jesus. Same thing." I needed the laugh.

She hung up. I realized I'd deliberately left out

114

one key element in the story, one that would be particularly important to an AA sponsor, and called back. "I didn't tell you, we're having sex."

"Safer sex?" Mara asked automatically.

"Of course. At least we were. It's been on the back burner since all this shit started to happen."

"Honey, after all you've told me, I'd say your first worry is staying alive! We'll worry about that aspect of the relationship later, okay?"

"Thanks a lot, Mara," I said with sarcasm dripping from my voice.

"You're welcome," she said sweetly. We both hung up for the second time.

Damn that woman.

It had been a while since I'd checked in at Samms', and I made tentative arrangements to join Carmen's family on Labor Day at noon for a gigantic cookout, promising to bring plenty of my famous turkey salad, made with water chestnuts, celery, almonds, mayonnaise and curry. I'd gotten the recipe from the *Times* one year faced with leftovers from a Thanksgiving turkey. Carmen would bring the extras from the picnic to the bar at six for a holiday potluck dinner for all our customers. I wasn't sure if Hayley would want to go over to the bar after the cookout, or even if she should, but at least I'd planned something for the holiday itself.

Hayley emerged from her nap and said a proper hello to Max and Frank. She scarfed down the rest of the chicken and made another pitcher of lemonade from the ripe lemons on the kitchen windowsill. We sipped from frosty glasses in silence. Waiting.

At eleven we went inside the guesthouse to watch the day's news on television. I felt as if I'd been on a desert island for three days. Max went back to the main house to sleep in Hayley's room. I suspected she had a knife or small gun from the way she kept checking her pants pocket, but I didn't want to know.

I let Radar make her evening run — on three legs — to the pea gravel while Frank was commanded to sit, then Frank got the run of the yard for the night. I couldn't imagine anyone daring that hulking monster's fangs.

Apparently no one did. Max bid us good-bye at six-thirty in the morning to go to work, and we sat on the deck, accompanied by hulking Frank, until Val arrived.

Our uniformed bodyguard checked the premises and exterior wall and found nothing new. The three of us sat, walked, chatted and killed time until Val had to leave.

We got a call at nine that a night-shift bodyguard had been found and she could start at midnight. The three of us waited up for her and briefed her before hitting the sack, the same sleeping arrangements as the night before. In the morning Val informed us that a third woman had been found to take over the four-to-midnight shift. We now had round-the-clock protection.

Hayley and I sat around the pool all day, wearing suits from Kitt's extensive collection. Everywhere we went I could imagine unseen eyes focused on us. Hayley took a turn making spaghetti — more comfort food — timing it for Max's arrival. We ate silently. The presence of the armed bodyguard sitting by the pool was distracting as well as reassuring.

116

"I might as well go on home," Max said. "You don't need me now. Besides, it would be too easy to get used to digs like this."

"I bet you have to check on that somebody you were with the first time I called," I said.

"Can't keep nothin' from you," she admitted. We hugged each other, Hayley offered her a distant handshake, and Max and her monster dog drove away. Hayley and I slept on the futon again while the midnight bodyguard stood watch outside.

Val came on duty at eight. I felt like Princess Di as the changing of the guard kept outsiders out but kept her imprisoned as well. This was getting old.

CHAPTER TWELVE

It got even older as the rest of the week and weekend played out. Each bodyguard vigilantly checked all doors and windows and the entire grounds every hour. Several of Kitt's employees from her West Hollywood offices came by to pick up materials from her office and from my bedroom/ storage room. Like wardens, the bodyguards escorted them around. We tried to put on the other security systems but had the same problems as before — so many unsettling false alarms that we gave up on them.

Hayley asked to be taken to McCabe's Guitar Store in West L.A., where she played every guitar in the shop before selecting one. She tried to explain its finer features but I know nothing about music beyond what I hear on the jukebox and in concerts. Even working for Kitt hasn't helped much.

Back home, Hayley played with her new instrument for a while before asking me to call Kitt. "I need to pay her for all of this extra protection," she said. "Find out how much it is."

Over the phone Kitt downplayed the cost.

"I think she really wants to pay her own way." I relayed the message I was getting from Hayley. "She knows this is adding up every day this goes on."

"So, okay, let her pay if she wants. No matter to me, just so she stays there where she's safe and we can keep a watch on her."

"Maybe I should move out and let you two get your lives back to normal," Hayley said in the background, loudly enough for Kitt to hear.

"*No way*! You tell her that she's in the safest place she can be."

"Tell her yourself," I said, putting Hayley on the line. The two of them went at it but the gist of the final agreement was that Hayley would stay until all of us found out who this stalker, or ghost, really was. I could see relief in Hayley's eyes as she hung up.

Monday came, and we invited Val, already on time and a half because of the Labor Day holiday, to come along with us and let the security force check the house. "What a job, paid to party," she joked. We put her in one of my navy silk blouses and a long vest that hid her holster; the navy uniform slacks never looked better.

We'd had a mini-Thanksgiving feast Sunday and I took my turkey salad made with the leftovers to Carmen's. Her blue house sits on stilts in a Highland Park hillside neighborhood. Carmen got her sister and brother out of Honduras the moment she became a U.S. citizen, and their two families were there as well.

Little kids ran underfoot, squealing and screaming, dribbling mustard down their shirts, teasing Carmen's dachshund till the poor thing hid under the huge poster bed. Nancy Jefferson, my other full-time bartender, and Jerry Rodriguez, one of my part-time bouncers/bartenders, were also there with their lovers.

Carmen, in her usual New York-inspired all-black clothes, was cooking cabrito, a roast young goat. She'd gotten a buzz haircut herself and teased Hayley about wearing a hat indoors. "You're hiding your crowning glory," Carmen said.

"Yeah, sure, your black hair looks a lot better in a buzz than my peach fuzz," Hayley retorted. Finally she took off her kufi and laid it on a chair.

Carmen's sister was putting together yellow rice, black beans and other Honduran side dishes, and her brother had hot dogs on the barbecue for the kids. Nancy brought a huge macaroni-and-tuna salad, Jerry had made buckets of coleslaw and fried chicken.

Val worried that she should have brought

something. "Don't be ridiculous," we told her. There would be plenty of food for the bar party that night.

We ate like fiends, slurping and complimenting one another. Carmen's brother discreetly hid his beer from view, in deference to Hayley. The rest of us glugged soft drinks. Hayley relaxed in the congenial crowd and played children's songs on her guitar for the kids.

"Anything except Barney — I barf for Barney," she told them. They thought this was hilarious and ran around the house singing, "I love you, you love me," with throw-up sounds between every phrase. The kids thought it was funny a lot longer than the grown-ups did. All of us joined in on "This Land Is Your Land" and "Michael Row the Boat Ashore." An All-American Labor Day.

Carmen made a point of getting me to agree to come by the bar the next night, my birthday, for a little party. At least she hadn't forgotten. I said I'd have to arrange it with the bodyguard who'd be on that shift.

"You have to come with us tonight, too, to carry all this food," Carmen insisted. I had to check with Hayley, who was still playing tunes for the kids.

"How do you feel about going to Samms' tonight?" I asked.

"I feel great," she shrugged. "As long as I feel safe, being in a bar's not going to tempt me to drink. Just don't stick a bottle of cherry wine in my hand."

"Promise, no cherry wine." I smiled. I slipped away and asked Carmen to make sure nothing resembling cherry wine would be in evidence anywhere in the bar that night.

We walked into Samms' around eight to find all the lights were out. Strange. Even more weird, the parking lot was jammed. "What's going on?" I said. "Val? You're still on duty?" We tiptoed to the door and eased in. Hayley took a moment to plant her kufi firmly on her head; that should have been a clue.

"*Surprise!*" a crowd yelled, flashing the lights off and on, then switching to the strobes to make everybody blind. A twenty-foot banner proclaimed, "Happy 50th Birthday, Laney!" They had my favorite cake, a gigantic white sheet cake from Phoenix Bakery in Chinatown with whipped cream frosting and filling and fresh strawberries all over the top.

"I thought you said to come by tomorrow night for a party," I accused a smug Carmen.

"Gotcha," she said.

Some fool had ordered black helium-filled balloons in the shape of tombstones, with the inscription "R.I.P.-Youth."

"You'll pay for this." I laughed at the sight of the balloons. "Somebody who came into the bar once said that her office threw her a party for her fiftieth birthday and they had these same 'R.I.P.' balloons. She had a heart attack the next day!"

"No, no, take them away," Nancy yelled. "No heart attack. You've got to live to a ripe old age."

"She's ripe, all right," Max quipped, making as if to sniff in my direction. True class.

"Eighty-six that woman," I ordered, making a slicing motion at my throat. We all laughed and had a great time, Hayley taking part in the surprise party as if she'd been in on the planning. I told her as much.

"I was," she said, eyes sparkling from the bar's overhead mirrored light-reflector. "Carmen wanted to make sure you'd come tonight, looking halfway decent. I fussed and took up time so we'd get here around eight. And don't you remember I had to tell you to wear something besides that faded Sue Fink T-shirt?"

By gosh, she had. So it was no coincidence that I was in my favorite steel-blue jumpsuit, and that Hayley's kufi matched all the primary colors in her print shirt that was slit to the waist in front, over yellow leggings.

We talked and danced for a couple of hours, Hayley doing a wild shimmy in that shirt, revealing flashes of breast to one and all. She danced with everybody but saved the slow ones for me. I saw the whispers going round over that. New customers quickly heard that the show-off was Hayley Malone, and if they needed to be reminded who that was, well, the whispers soon brought them up to snuff.

"Sing something, Hayley," more and more people began to ask.

"Well, why the hell not?" Hayley announced. She sent Nancy to the car for her guitar, and we turned off the jukebox. Samms' has a stage where we bring in a band once in a while, and Carmen supervised the rearrangement of chairs and tables.

Hayley took her place on a transported bar stool.

It took her a long time to check her tuning, while everyone in the bar waited patiently. She let loose with Tina Turner's signature hit, "Proud Mary." She made her whole body and head shake like Turner and her kufi flew off. Her hands flew to her scalp, her guitar heading for the floor. Immediately she caught the guitar. "What the hell," she said, breaking back into the lyrics as if nothing had happened. The soft peach fuzz, like a baby's hair, was an innocent contrast to her revealing shirt.

"Lookin' good, Hayley," someone yelled.

"Yeah?" She looked up in wonderment.

Max wolf-whistled and stomped her boots. Others followed. Hayley threw back her head and chortled. She launched into a medley of Janis Joplin hits that took the crowd to fever pitch. She followed with several other popular tunes, but not a note from any of her own songs.

"Whew, I'm exhausted, folks, can't sing another note," she apologized.

The cheers and applause were louder than for any act I'd ever brought to Samms'. But then, she'd been better than any act I'd ever brought to Samms'. Far better. She still had it. Max shook a bottle of Perrier and let it fizz all over Hayley's sweaty face.

"Thanks — I guess." Hayley laughed, wiping herself off with a bar towel I offered. "I'm out of shape in more ways than one," she said when her breathing returned to normal. "We've got to get back to jogging, Laney."

"Ready when you are," I said. "Val, you up to jogging?"

"Are you kidding." Val snorted, flashing a bicep

and slapping her hard thigh. "I do three miles a day, rain or shine."

The realization of why we had Val there in the first place sobered my exhilaration. Did we dare go jogging outside our safe compound? "Maybe you can suggest some exercises we can do at home to get in shape," I said. "Or maybe we should just swim more."

"Best exercise there is," Val agreed. The jukebox was back on and couples were dancing again. Max shooed away the few patrons who were insistent about approaching Hayley again, telling them Hayley needed her rest.

Val found the ubiquitous kufi and rounded up Hayley and me and got us to her car. "Enough for one day," she pronounced. Back on Mount Washington, she checked with the evening shift bodyguard and left, shaking her head and muttering, "To think I got paid overtime for this!"

"Ready for your own room yet?" I asked Hayley.

"I still want to sleep with you." We both grinned at the irony of that statement; neither of us had thought of sex since the break-in. Tentatively we kissed. Too much worry and tension whirled around between us. It would wait.

She put on her old oversized white shirt to sleep in. As if tucking in a child, I pulled a fresh comforter around her.

Radar limped out to the pea gravel and did her business before returning to her own comforter. I shut the doggie door to keep her in for the night. "We have a human bodyguard with a gun trying to replace you," I said to the shepherd, giving her a hug. "She costs a lot more than dog food too."

She whimpered and gave her cast a nibble.

"Uh uh, girl, leave it alone." She licked my chin. "Good dog. I know it's hard on you, and I miss you too," I assured her. "We'll have good times again, I promise. Today was almost a normal day!" I slid under the covers next to Hayley and slept.

CHAPTER THIRTEEN

Kitt came back Wednesday and we reevaluated the situation. "Nothing else has happened, right?" she asked. Despite her constant sunscreen, she was deeply tanned from the cruise. She slathered her face with moisturizer as we sat outside on her second-floor balcony.

"Not a thing. None of the bodyguards or the security police have been able to find anything unusual except those broken branches that day," I said. Sipping a Diet Pepsi, I stared at the Pacific on the far horizon, mesmerized as usual by the promises the ocean always seems to be offering.

"I'm wondering whether we need to continue the bodyguards around the clock, now that there are three of us," Kitt interrupted my daydreams. "Frankly, I don't think anything's going to happen while the bodyguards are around. What do you think, Hayley?"

"It could be months before anything else happens," she said. "Sometimes it's years." She was scribbling furiously in a notebook, humming to herself. Good sign, I thought.

"And maybe we *want* something else to happen, to get this over once and for all. Are you up to it, Hayley?" Kitt asked.

Hayley nodded. I wondered. "Are you sure you're strong enough to handle whatever might come up?" I asked.

"I want this over with, one way or another," she said, her pen gouging into the paper.

"Whadda ya say, ex the bodyguards? For now?" Kitt's question was to both of us, and we both agreed.

We decided to have an impromptu farewell party for Val, defrosting shrimp and chicken breasts for a barbecue. Kitt had brought home a bottle of a new gourmet lime-cilantro-ginger sauce from an airport shop in Miami and wanted to try it. She licked her sunburned lips as she sliced the chicken and poured the chunky green marinade over it. I fired up the grill.

"So now I have a new addiction and I have to travel to Miami to feed it." She sighed, polishing off the last tangy shrimp. "Val, we're going to miss you and your co-workers. If we need you again, promise you'll be available."

"For you, anything," Val said, heading for her car. We waved good-bye and the three of us were left alone on the property. Suddenly I felt very vulnerable.

"Not too late to call her back," Kitt mused, apparently feeling the same thing. Hayley gave a small shiver.

"We'll be fine, now that there's three of us again," I stated more firmly than I felt.

Kitt said, "Hmmm." We sat around for a while, the tension palpable. "Okay, bodyguards back, or just a fourth body?" We agreed that just another person around would feel better.

The next day, Kitt made a phone call to one of her employees at the West Hollywood office. "Adrienne, you live alone, right? How'd you like to spend a week or two at my house on Mount Washington? At extra pay, of course. I could use a transcriptionist here, help me organize my files at home." She paused.

"Yes, yes, it's partly because I want another body in the house while Hayley's here. Yes, you can use the pool. You will? Great, go home and pack and we'll see you here ASAP."

So we had a fourth person living with us for two weeks, during which time nothing else happened. Oh, somebody who had been at my birthday party apparently knew somebody at the *Hollywood Reporter*, because there was a mention in one of the columns about how Hayley Malone was back in town, singing greater than ever, and how her last stay at Betty Ford's had "done the trick." Kitt had to divert a few calls around that one, Hayley insisting that she was in no way ready for another attempted "comeback."

Adrienne, a lanky blond prone to pouring on black catsuits, organized and reorganized every file in the place and even categorized the materials in the guesthouse office. Finally she tired of sitting around Mount Washington while the West Hollywood office called her constantly for help, and she went home to Los Feliz. The three of us were alone again. And nothing more happened.

It began to feel as if we could get back to "normal," whatever that might be — all the while knowing that sometime, someplace, somehow, something or someone could jump back into our lives in some unimaginable way. I began to appreciate how Hayley must have felt all those years, not knowing when the next shoe would drop.

Hayley and I started to jog around Mount Washington again, once Radar's cast came off and she could keep up with us. Hayley even attended a weekly AA meeting with me. I began to make my rounds of my public relations customers, sending out their newsletters regularly again.

Hayley was writing new songs and occasionally she let me hear one when she felt it was near completion. To be honest, she didn't have her own style anymore; her lyrics were trite. That's what had come across on that Johnny Carson show years ago. I wondered what it would take for Hayley to be able to write songs of the quality of "We're All Hurting" again. To relax, she clowned around with other people's hits, and at that she was a wonder.

She took a drive with me one day when I'd

gotten a big check from a client. First I made a few phone calls to friends to try to find a Jeep salesperson who was a lesbian. I tried to support the community, especially on big purchases. The closest I came was a woman in Glendale who had treated a lesbian couple fairly when they were car shopping. So Hayley and I drove to Glendale and test drove several models. The saleswoman met our approval — she told Hayley she liked her buzz.

"Which color do you want?" Hayley asked me after we'd seen every Cherokee on the lot and liked them all.

"White's been the most popular color for years, but green is the newest, trendiest color," the sales rep reported.

"That rules out those two," I joked.

"Right, you don't want trendy but you're buying a Jeep Cherokee," Hayley teased me.

I pretended not to hear her. "How about that blue one?" I motioned toward a car in the corner.

"BVM blue," Hayley said approvingly.

"Huh?"

"Blessed Virgin Mary blue. Remember the color of the robes on the statues? Weren't you raised Catholic too?"

She was right, the little 4x4 V-6 Jeep Cherokee Sport was exactly that color, a brighter, cleaner blue than anything else I'd seen on a car lately. "Spinnaker blue" was the official color.

"Good choice, it's a demo from last year with only a couple thousand miles on it, and it's loaded to the gills. I can give you a really great deal," the saleswoman said. With the price of new cars these days, I was glad to chance upon a demo, the cheapest Cherokee in the line to boot. It drove nicely too, with enough power to make it up even Baxter Hill, and enough room to seat six plus a ton of luggage. My poor old faded blue S-10 looked pathetic next to the Sport.

"I'll take it," I announced.

Rather than deal with the hassles of selling the S-10 myself in an attempt to get a better price, I took the trade-in value offered on it. The L.A. economy is so bad that I got a steal overall.

Having a new car gave me a lift. I used every excuse to get out and drive, Hayley laughing at my side much of the time. The demo could play both CDs and cassettes, and the two of us drove to Santa Barbara one day along the Pacific Coast Highway, a hundred-mile delight, just to have lunch on the pier.

And still nothing happened. We almost began to breathe again.

I was aware that Hayley and I had become more like sisters, with neither of us seemingly interested in anything sexual, and that was okay too. In some ways it was a relief.

It was mid-October when Kitt had to leave California for a few days on business. At this point we didn't even think about bringing in a third person for the duration. It was as if nothing ever *had* happened.

My throat was raspy the second morning that Kitt had been gone, and I decided to pass on the morning jog. "That's okay. Radar'll go with me," Hayley said, grabbing my teal Samms' Sluggers sweatshirt and her old baseball cap as she left. I found a jar of Vick's VapoRub and headed for the shower to try and fend off the cold I knew was coming.

Letting the hot water stream out for a few minutes first, while the VapoRub aroma filled the bathroom and fogged the mirrors, I shaved off the few straggly hairs that had started to grow on my chin. I'd seen Anne go through menopause ahead of me, so I wasn't shocked at these new wiry protrusions.

On principle, Anne hadn't shaved her armpits or legs since the late sixties, but she sure attacked each new whisker, and so do I. Next will probably be the damned hot flashes that had bothered Anne so much for a while.

The medicinal steam was loosening the congestion in my chest that I hadn't quite realized was there. I took a nail file from the medicine chest and smoothed a fingernail while I deliberately breathed deeply. Finally I stripped off my terrycloth robe, pushed aside the white plastic shower curtain, and eased into the wet heat.

The pounding droplets felt good against my shoulders and back, which had that feeling of pending achiness, just borderline, not enough for Advil yet.

Cursing a bar of Dial that slipped out of my hands, I bent over and felt for it on the bathtub floor. "Where the hell are you?" I muttered before finding the bar, straightening up and rubbing soap from my eyes.

The shadows in the room were different than a second ago.

Suddenly the shower curtain twisted and a gloved hand grabbed my arm and yanked it behind my back with such force that I expected to hear bones snap. A piece of metal, a garden tool, something with five arrow-sharp prongs, hurtled toward my face. I ducked and pulled the man down with me.

Wrestling on the bathtub floor, he got me in the abdomen with the tool and again in my thigh. The pain caught my breath and paralyzed me. I could see blood flowing, spurting everywhere. The shower curtain was a living mosaic of red and pink rivulets. Through the curtain I caught a glimpse of a face. Hayley's rapist.

My old anti-rape training kicked in. Ripping the shower curtain off its plastic rings, I grabbed my right hand with my left to make it strong and aimed my fingers at what I thought were eye sockets, as best I could see through the steam and the soapy water burning my eyes. The shape yelled and slapped me across the face, hard.

"Bitch, I'll get you for that," said the male voice. Hands reached for me, slipped off the soap.

I struggled to my feet. He attempted to follow. I used my foot to pull his leg out from under him and send him to the floor of the tub again. His head hit the faucet hard.

Uncertain on my feet in the wet tub, the shower curtain twisted around one leg, I still chanced a kick to his groin. The thrust landed hard enough that he doubled up. I jumped out of the tub and turned on the hot water as high as it would go, sending scalding steam shooting over his T-shirted back. He yelled and tried to get up again, this time succeeding. Before he could escape I reached for the shampoo bottle to break it for a weapon but it was soft plastic. I shot the contents in his face. The bottle gasped the last of its suds. Now he was blinded too.

I reached around me for a weapon and found the nail file and plastic razor on the back of the toilet. I slashed furiously in the direction of the man's face with the razor in one hand and jabbed the sharp metal point of the file all over at him with the other, ripping his shirt to shreds, while emitting a throaty yell that sounded more like a furious grizzly than a frightened woman.

I was most afraid of slipping on the wet bathroom floor as he groped for me and tried to pull me down. He succeeded and I dropped the razor and nail file as I fell, but I grabbed for his balls as I plummeted. Through denim I made contact with a lump and squeezed with all my power. He shrieked, doubled over again, then struggled to his feet. He stomped on my shinbone as he escaped, running bent over like a chimpanzee.

I reached for the ceramic toilet brush holder and hurled it at his retreating back. It bounced off and landed unbroken on the carpet but I knew it had to leave a bruise. The bloody garden tool was in the tub — I threw it too, but missed. It took a framed print off the wooden wall with it when it fell and left a red smear down the pine.

I cleared my eyes and saw a glimpse of white T-shirt, jeans, brown crew cut disappearing out my poolside door. Definitely Hayley's ghost, the rapist. The metal security screen door clanged in its jamb.

Now I could let myself be scared. *My God, I'm bleeding to death.*

Quickly I pressed towels tightly against my thigh and abdomen where two lines of five punctures each indicated where the tool had hit. Two of the wounds spouted bright red blood, another oozed a darker color, the others were just puddles. Tripping over the ripped shower curtain, I broke loose, raced to the phone and dialed 911 for an ambulance, all the while trying to keep the compression on the wounds, particularly the spot inside my thigh and the one near my groin which were bleeding the hardest.

An ambulance could take forever to come, winding its way up Mount Washington. It would be quicker to drive myself, but I didn't dare chance it. How much blood could I lose before passing out? While I paced, pressing against the arteries in a life-lock, I tried to think of what else should be done. Automatically I turned off the pounding hot water still spewing in the tub. My heartbeat pounded in my ears as if supercharged.

I called Kitt's office and told them I'd probably be taken to Big County because it was the closest hospital with a trauma center and to tell Kitt and tell Carmen and tell Hayley when she got back from her run . . .

As I talked furiously, trying to cover all contingencies, my wet body started to chill. My teeth chattered as I kept talking. I felt like I was on automatic pilot, and involuntarily my feet started to make little jumping steps in place. Adrienne was shouting on the other end of the phone, then a calmer voice I couldn't place took over and tried to reassure me. "Stay calm, Laney," someone said, over and over.

"I *am* calm," I insisted, over and over back at her.

I didn't want to let go of the telephone lifeline until the ambulance came, but I was freezing, longing for the white terrycloth robe in the bathroom. My dancing increased in speed. I could see the circle of water and blood widening on the floor around me.

Hayley came through the guesthouse door humming to herself. She saw me and screamed.

CHAPTER FOURTEEN

She collapsed and went into shock — I could see her face grow clammy and pale. Radar barked helplessly, circling us both. On my hands and knees, still holding my wounds tightly to stem the bleeding, I moved her to the rug and got the comforter up around her. I could hear a siren coming up Mount Washington drive, behind Radar's frantic barking. I wanted to go check outside. Don't move, I told myself, keep the compression on the blood vessels.

The ambulance was stopped at the security gate.

I had to go outside anyway and let it through. First I let go of my towel bandages long enough to put on the robe. Ruined, I thought idly as I contemplated the soaked towels. They were my new peach ones, too.

The paramedics hoisted Hayley onto a gurney that matched the one for me and slid both of us into the rear of the ambulance. I made one paramedic go around with the keys and deadbolt all the doors, leaving Radar solely in charge.

The paramedic said he didn't see the shepherd attacking anybody, just barking up at a section of the fence. I couldn't do anymore. The paramedics threatened me with a sedative if I didn't just lie down and stay calm. The ambulance bed was hard, the ride jarring. This was no way to treat a sick person. Suddenly I couldn't do anything *but* lie down and stay calm. I was out cold.

When I awakened, Hayley was sitting by my side, chatting in broken Spanish with a woman in the bed next to me about how the woman should leave her husband now that he'd dislocated her shoulder.

"Laney! You're awake!" She gave me a big hug. It hurt. I couldn't hug back. I hurt all over. I pulled off the covers and lifted my gown. What caught my eye first was my left shin, as purple as a plum. Welts on my right forearm matched it. Bandages covered much of my thigh and stomach and the joint between. I hurt.

"What happened?" I asked. "Are you okay?"

"Yeah, I recovered in the ambulance. Seeing you and all that blood was a shock, that's all."

I took that statement in. What was she talking about? "What happened?" I repeated. My head was woozy. Pain pills at work. Or rather, not at work, not enough. I searched for the buzzer to summon a nurse.

"That's what I wanted to ask *you!*" She handed me the rubber tubing with the buzzer on the end. I hit it over and over again, somehow expecting that a nurse would actually appear.

"I'm in Big County, right?"

Hayley nodded. "It's Wednesday." It would be a long wait for medication.

I sighed. I'd been in just over twenty-four hours.

"Before you tell *me* what happened, I'd better tell you that the LAPD is involved," Hayley said. "The paramedics reported it as an obvious break-in and assault, and since there were injuries, there had to be a report. I told them I wasn't there, I didn't know anything, they'd have to talk to you. What'll we tell them?"

It was hard to concentrate, but the memories were coming back.

"Oh, and I gave them a phony name. For me, that is. I'm Allison Chambers, a friend of yours just visiting. Kitt's office hasn't been able to reach her yet but I told them the same thing, so we should be able to keep this out of the papers. It's just another minor assault, in the cops' eyes, as long as my name isn't mentioned."

"Chambers, right. Same name you used last June. Any reason for it?"

"No, I just like the sound of it. I use it a lot."

"Okay, so how long have you been staying with me, Allison?" From the comfort of my bed I felt as protective of her as a mother cat with her kitten in her mouth, looking for a safe nest. A kicked cat.

"I said a month. I'm going through a divorce and moved in with friends to get myself together."

"God, I hate lies. I can never remember who I told what. Okay, that much sounds simple enough. Anything else?"

"No, that's all . . . and a good thing too. Hi, Officer Powell," she greeted the man at the door. Bimbo, her posture and gestures indicated, I'm only the bimbo here. She'd brought the pink scarf to add to her innocent look. She sat arched in her hospital plastic stacking chair so that her Vicki Randle T-shirt showed off her breasts. Powell never seemed to look at her face.

As I was able to focus, I realized how nervous she seemed compared to normal, or at least as "normal" as I'd ever seen her. Naturally she'd be nervous. Somebody had just tried to kill her, but they'd gotten me instead. I'd have to change my report around so that there was no indication that she was the real target. More lies, I worried.

He ignored Hayley/Allison, the bimbo act apparently working, and took only a few facts from me in his cursory report. Five-ten, male Caucasian, around forty, jeans and white T-shirt. No scars that I could see.

Glancing at Hayley, I wondered if the description was making her "ghost" seem very real and dangerous, and she was trying to hide it by remaining absolutely still. Too still for Hayley.

"Could you see his shoes?"

"Umm, white tennis shoes, the cheap, no-brand kind. Not high tops, nothing fancy. Umm, red laces!"

Hayley noticeably jumped. At least it was noticeable to me. Powell stared at his forms.

"I remember being on the floor of the shower and seeing my blood splash on his shoes and thinking how it matched his bows. It was kind of funny in a giddy sort of way."

"Anything else out of the ordinary?"

"I remember that the back of his neck was deeply tanned and wrinkled, like he was outside a lot. Funny the little things you remember later."

"That's why we're talking to you," the policeman said, sounding bored. "Hair color?"

"Brown. Tree-bark brown."

"Tree-bark brown." The cop printed slowly, his sarcasm etched in with each deliberate letter.

"It was like an old-fashioned crew cut, not the sleek new kind. Kind of thatchy all around. Not punk either. Like an old Jerry Lewis movie."

"Crew cut," Powell repeated, ignoring my amplifications.

I squeezed my eyes shut. A flash of turquoise. "Oh, and he had some sort of fancy belt buckle, something turquoise, maybe like an Indian design. His T-shirt must have been tucked in for me to see the buckle. The belt was dark, maybe black leather, but real worn so you could see the white coming through in spots."

Hayley was frozen in place. I debated offering her a glass of water to get her to move a little, but decided she'd probably drop it. Anyway, Powell still didn't seem to notice.

"Point of entry?"

I had to think carefully to avoid giving away anything I didn't want to. It would be safe to report what I had originally told the security force when Hayley first moved in, since they never were given the full story, only the bodyguards were.

"We've been having some trouble with somebody coming over the fence, and we've informed our private security force to be on the lookout. I guess the intruder managed to time his break-in between their drive-bys," I said.

"Any reason why he would be after you?"

"Interrupted robbery, probably. We have a lot of electronic stuff and CDs at the house," I told him. "Easy-to-fence stuff."

I was ready to blame the attack on the drug lab incident if pressed further. A good cop would wonder why a robber would come into the shower and interrupt his own crime. A good cop would have ordered a blood analysis of the nail file and razor I'd used on the guy. I made a mental note to put the two items in a plastic baggie and keep it in the fridge.

A good cop would know by now that Hayley/ Allison had gone off wearing my distinctive teal sweatshirt with a cap over her hair, with my dog, so no one could tell it wasn't me, at least from a distance. A good cop would see that Hayley/Allison was in obvious distress and wonder what he was not being told. A good cop would have asked every detail of those previous trespassings. Powell was not a good cop.

We discussed security precautions further, Officer Powell apparently having a standard monologue to

143

be delivered in robbery cases. I listened politely. His radio crackled and he answered it and rushed off without a good-bye. An attempted murder-suicide on DeSoto, I think I heard. Who can be bothered with a break-in and minor injuries when the city is full of unsolved murders? I was fairly sure we'd never hear from Officer Powell again.

"Whew, what a geek," Hayley said once he was out of the room.

"What's up, Hayley?"

"What do you mean, what's up?"

"Just that — what hit you so hard about this guy wearing a crew cut and a T-shirt with a pack of cigarettes rolled up in the sleeve and a turquoise belt buckle and red shoe laces?"

"Nothing. I mean, I don't know. I just got the chills when I heard your description. It was like warning bells went off somewhere in my head, but somebody immediately jumped on the bells and silenced them. Honestly, I have no idea who this guy is."

"Are you sure you don't know? Hayley, it was the same guy who raped you last June."

She went pale. For a moment I thought she would vomit.

"Oh, my God. It's Len. Len, Len, Len, Len." Her white lips stuttered as if she were freezing. "Len Hunsaker. I killed Len Hunsaker. He's the ghost!" She slumped in her chair and landed on the floor in a heap.

Yet another collapse. I felt numb, unable to cope with her distress, though moments earlier I'd felt confident of my ability to protect her. From somewhere, I remembered reading about fainting goats, who keel over at the slightest shock. They're bred by sheep owners who put them in their flocks to keep attacking coyotes and wolves occupied while the more valuable sheep escape. If Hayley had been the one in the shower, she'd be dead right now.

I should have been calling for the nurse. My voice wouldn't work. I tried to find the call button on the end of the rubber tube, but it was flopping somewhere on the floor.

No need, the woman in the bed next to me was shouting. Nurses were arriving from every direction. I only hoped my neighbor's English comprehension and hearing had been as bad as Hayley's Spanish. Who the hell was Len Hunsaker?

CHAPTER FIFTEEN

Hayley sat up and assured everyone that she was fine, just fine. It was only the aftershocks from the break-in and her friend being hurt. No, she didn't need further treatment herself.

The woman next to me wasn't calling for the cops — she merely looked relieved; she obviously hadn't heard or understood the murder confession. I wasn't sure what I'd heard, either. Hayley had murdered somebody? And now she was coolly deflecting medical attention.

Hayley certainly knew how to put on a pretty

good act. She could play bimbo, crazy lady, drunkard, dominatrix or Janis Joplin at the flutter of a lash. The thought did a hairpin turn: had she been playing me?

"Time for you to go on home and recuperate, Mrs. Samms," a nurse said, paperwork in hand. Why correct her? What difference did it make in the grand scheme of things? If I said, "You are mistaken. I am a lesbian and therefore not going to give up my identity to become a Mrs. anybody." Would my coming out really hasten the grand day of equality? Probably. I was too tired.

"You wouldn't be needing my bed for an attempted murder-suicide being rushed here now, would you?" I asked in innocence. Her eyes narrowed, but she kept up her line. "We only keep sick folks here, and you're doing fine. Check in with the cashier when you leave."

Glad as I was to get out of there, I wondered if I would have gotten the boot anyway even if I'd had something seriously wrong. In L.A., it's hard not to be suspicious.

Turned out that I'd needed only one pint of blood to go with the fine stitching done by a microvascular surgeon on the severed arteries. My uterus and intestine had been nicked; thanks to modern surgical techniques they'd been repaired through only tiny openings. Stitches were to stay in for two more weeks. I was to check with my personal physician the next day and follow his advice on how to continue caring for my wounds.

"His," naturally. I had a her, a gynecologist, but I'd have to ask Kitt for the name of a GP. No problem, Kitt would have recommendations for any crisis. Maybe even for a murder confession from her trusted Hayley.

Back home Radar jumped up on both of us and ran around us in tight circles until she was sure we were both okay. Hayley and I sat outside with the everpresent fresh lemonade, Hayley tucking herself into the lawn chair and hugging her legs close to her body. As soon as I could, I quizzed her about Len Hunsaker.

"I don't know, the name just popped up. I keep getting bits and pieces of more memories. God, I thought I was through with this," she said, rocking her body back and forth in her chair like an autistic child.

"So what exactly did you remember?"

"It was strange, it was like there was a wall of gray shrubs, more like fog, and suddenly a shape materialized in the fog and it was a man and it had a name. Len Hunsaker."

Strange name.

"He had on a white T-shirt with a red and white pack of Lucky Strikes rolled up in the sleeve. I remember a fancy silver and turquoise belt buckle, faded jeans, and white tennis shoes with red laces. I don't know where the name came from or anything else, except I am absolutely certain that I killed him. And I don't have the faintest idea how or when or why."

We tossed ideas back and forth. Nothing else came to her. Now we really had unanswered questions.

Staring at my bandages, I decided to believe her. This time, somebody had wanted to kill her because they couldn't drive her to drink. That person or persons undoubtedly still wanted to kill her. It would be enough to make anyone a little schizoid.

I couldn't get any of the same bodyguards on short notice, so I begged Max to come back with Frank, her Rottweiler, until we could get round-the-clock protection again. With Radar up and around, the two dogs met as equals and he didn't try to attack her.

Max had bought a handgun in the interim, a simple .38 Smith & Wesson pistol, a "Lady Smith," if you can believe it, aimed at the female market, and my gratitude outweighed my distaste for guns. I wouldn't have minded one of the old M-16s we trained on in the Army. I use the term "trained" loosely — no one ever dreamed back then that a woman in the military might actually have to fire a gun sometime.

Max had never fired her gun and barely knew how to load it. Exactly the kind of armed home-owner the cops warn us against. Exactly the kind who is far more likely to get shot with her own weapon than to use it on an assailant. At least she'd registered it. I experimented with the pistol until I could load smoothly. I wished I could get to a range to practice. I wished I had a license to carry.

In my records I dug up the name of the Detroit private investigator I'd hired years ago to look for my mother. He was dead but the firm went on, and I put another PI on the task of checking out everything about a Len Hunsaker. He had to have a Michigan connection somewhere, probably around the time of Hayley's mother's miscarriage in 1959.

As I unlocked the security door to my guesthouse, a picture flashed in my head: the same door ajar after the rapist's hasty exit. The lock unbroken. He had to have had a key. I ordered new locks on all the security doors throughout the estate and kept the duplicates on my own key ring. No wonder he'd been able to come and go. But how had he gotten a key?

When I could reach Kitt she was shocked at the news but approving of all the decisions I had made so far. She promised to cut her trip short and be home in a few days, and she gave me the name of her GP.

Before Kitt got home from her business trip I had the PI's report. A Leonard Hunsaker had been born in Paw Paw, Michigan in 1941. He'd dropped out of high school there and worked briefly in St. Francis Winery, which, it turned out, produced dozens of award-winning wines, including a sweet cherry wine from Michigan's abundant crop.

"Yeah, that's it," Hayley said. "Now that I hear the name, I know it." Kitt had recalled a St. something from the Shell House incident as well. "But there were other brands too." Even an occasional Manischewitz.

Leonard Hunsaker had worked for Armstrong Dairy in Cadatunk near Bad Axe from 1957 to 1959, and then there was nothing more to be found on him anywhere in Michigan. No Social Security account — agricultural workers weren't covered under Social Security those days, a footnote to the report explained. No drivers' licenses from any U.S. state. The firm found no wedding licenses, no hunting licenses, no employment records — and no death or burial notices — for a Leonard Hunsaker anywhere in Michigan or California, though they'd keep checking other states. His parents were alive but had had no word of him since 1956. The PI indicated that the parents had not wanted to talk about why their son had gone out of their lives at age fifteen, and there had been nothing in the Paw Paw papers or records from that time to yield any clues.

"It's as if Len Hunsaker ceased to exist in nineteen fifty-nine," I mused aloud.

"I told you, I killed him," Hayley said.

"Then why wasn't there a death notice or a burial?" I wondered. A few minutes later I had come to a conclusion: "The only way we're going to find out what happened is to go to Michigan. It's the only way you're going to remember anything." Hayley cast me a wild-eyed look, then finally agreed.

Kitt's physician changed my bandages for a smaller variety. "Keep the wounds clean and dry, and come back in two weeks to get the stitches out." Time enough to get to Michigan and back.

Drive or fly to Michigan? I wanted to have Radar with us. With two of us driving we could make it in three days, four easy, and for some reason I wanted my own four-wheel-drive car with me in Michigan. I pictured bouncing over muddy, two-rut lanes to get to Hayley's old farm.

She laughed and said that country folks had paved roads just like city slickers, though she admitted that some gravel back roads could get pretty torn up by the monster tractors and multi-ton sugar beet trucks. "You just want to see how your Jeep does flat out," she joked. Had me there.

AAA suggested the best route to Michigan for late October. We couldn't chance the high route because there might be snow closing the mountain passes near Salt Lake City. So we'd take Highways 40, 44, 65 and 69, just four roads from Barstow all the way cross country and into the Michigan Thumb, where M-53 would take us directly to Bad Axe and Cadatunk. We plotted our path and packed heavy sweaters and socks to head East.

Should we have a bodyguard with us? I remembered Hayley's belief that nothing would happen when the bodyguards were around, and I wanted this thing to come to some sort of head and be done with. As a poor substitute, Max tucked her unloaded Lady Smith in its case along with her registration into my trunk before we left.

"Are you nuts?" I told her. "I don't think gun registrations are transferable, in which case I'd be illegally transporting a gun across state lines in a car. That's all we need."

"Not true. You can carry my gun as long as it's registered in some state somewhere," Max assured me. "You just have to carry it unloaded and locked in the trunk."

I called the state police and got various answers when I attempted to verify her statement, but somehow the officers seemed to be encouraging me, without actually saying so, or verifying it was legal.

"We can't be everywhere," said one officer who wouldn't give his name. "Maybe you might even be breaking the law in some state or another as you go cross country, but it's better to be tried by twelve than carried by six."

I couldn't believe that it was me, Laney Samms, who left the petite Lady Smith in my car. What exactly did I think would happen in Michigan anyway? Most likely we would merely drive around

Hayley's old haunts in Michigan until something triggered more memories that would resolve this problem once and for all. That was my primary goal.

As we drove, I tried to get Hayley to go over her Michigan memories in greater detail. She was blocked.

About the time we needed gas, I needed coffee, and the coffee break turned into dinner at a Union 76 truck stop/restaurant. The waitress gave us a choice of any three "sides" with our pork chops: fries, mashed, baked, scalloped, hash browns, stuffing, rice, hominy grits, creamed corn, baked beans, pintos or slaw. Then she recited the fourteen varieties of pie awaiting us for dessert. We weren't in L.A. anymore.

We drove past midnight, and when my eyes wouldn't stay open any more we tried to find a decent motel in a town that didn't know the meaning of the word. At first I thought we'd gotten a double-sized waterbed by mistake, but it was only the overly soft mattress. The only way it would hold both of us was if we jammed up against each other in the middle.

"I don't think I'm up for this much closeness," Hayley said. "I'm not feeling in the mood for cuddling anyway."

I slept on the sofa that night, and ordered twin beds at the motels the following nights.

Alternating two-hour driving shifts, we put in ten hours a day on the road rather than the fourteen I'd planned. Somehow we couldn't push any harder. We couldn't push away from the last cup of coffee at breakfast, from the last sip of Pepsi at dinner, clinging to our moments of inertia. It was like driving through molasses, an involuntary push-pull.

The fourth night's motel was in Imlay City, at the end of twenty-four-hundred miles of freeway. We exited I-69 at early dusk, plenty of time to drive the sixty miles up M-53 to Cadatunk and Bad Axe that night.

"I'd rather be fresh in the morning for whatever we're going to find out," Hayley said. I agreed. Sore from the cramped driving positions, we both popped two Advils at the motel and looked through the half-inch-thick phone book for restaurants.

We talked of many things over green chili burritos at a place called Nachos. According to a yellowed news clipping taped on the restaurant's wall, the restaurant belonged to a family of former migrant workers who'd settled in Imlay City generations before.

Eventually, the conversation turned to us.

CHAPTER SIXTEEN

Hayley sipped the Mexican chocolate that served as her dessert. "Have I told you how much I appreciate everything you're doing for me?"

"No, not really, but you've had other things on your mind." I ate the last tortilla chip. My dessert.

"I don't know why you're doing all of this. It's like I finally have someone who loves me enough, who loves me like a mother, who'll risk her own life for me, and yet I've only known you a short time. It's too soon to be love." She drawled out the last word, trivializing it, mocking it. As if it weren't important. Because it was too important to face openly. I knew that self-deception too.

I mimicked her. "Luu-uv, as you put it, has a lot of faces and sides. I can say I love you and mean it, though it's not quite the deep, forever-and-ever, match-made-in-heaven meaning. Not yet anyway."

"What meaning does it have then? *If* you were to actually say you love me, that is." She was teasing me, but I could see she was anxious for my answer. I struggled for the truth.

"Okay, starting from the beginning, it was just kind of fun. I didn't expect anything serious, and I made the assumption, rightly or wrongly, that because of your past, you didn't either."

She shrugged her shoulders in apparent agreement.

"When all of this other stuff started to happen, everything shifted. We were under attack, and I felt it as much as you. Getting sliced up made it real clear we're both in danger. Yes, I could split and probably lose the danger, but I'm involved now. I feel as if my life is entwined with yours, and I like it that way. I don't want the involvement to end, even though I have no illusions that you'd ever settle down to any kind of ordinary life." I hesitated. Was this me speaking? Yes, I meant these words: "I want monogamy at this point in my life, and I'm not sure you'd ever be interested in that kind of relationship."

There, I'd said it all. My heart wasn't beating at all, as far as I could tell, waiting to see what she'd say.

For the longest time she didn't say anything, just

sipped her hot chocolate and helped the waitress stack the rest of our dishes to take them away. When we were alone again, Hayley stared out the window before she spoke.

"Yeah, I'm starting to feel some real caring for you, and I'm seeing some hope somewhere ahead for us. Maybe. Part of me, the old, beaten-down part that gives up too easily, says it's no use, I'm doomed, this ghost or whatever will never leave me alone. It never has before. But maybe . . ."

I had to force my last question. "Could you ever be monogamous?"

Unexpectedly, she threw back her head and laughed. So hard that the waitress and even the cook in the back room came back out to see if something was wrong.

"We're fine," I waved them away. The cook looked at his wrist. We were keeping them from closing. I wouldn't leave until she answered my question.

"Honey, right about now I feel like I might never have sex again and it wouldn't bother me a bit. When, if, this whole thing is settled with the ghost or whatever it is, I just may kick back and learn to be myself, the real Hayley, whatever that is, and I sure don't think that the real Hayley is going to be fucking everything that moves anymore." She bit her lip and turned serious. "Yes, I think I can be monogamous. Right now that sounds like a real good idea. And yes, I'm not likely to turn into little Susie Homemaker and stay in one place forever, but I'm ripe for some of that anyway."

As she looked into my eyes I could see her face changing again to something I could only describe as sultry. The Lauren Bacall part of Bacall meets Madonna. She fed me the last half-spoonful of chocolate.

I had to add something else. "Hayley, I have to say that there are moments when I think you're totally crazy, that I doubt my own sanity for being involved with you. I don't see you as someone ready to fall back into drugs and alcohol any moment, though I wish you'd come to more meetings just for reinforcement. It's more like, sometimes you're really strong and outrageous, and then you sort of phase out. Sometimes I wonder if *I'm* crazy."

A grin spread over her face. "That only proves you're totally sane. I wish I could say the same thing about me. One therapist at Betty Ford says that I might have inherited a mild version of manic depression from my mother, not enough to have to control with lithium, but something to remember when *I* can't figure out what's going on."

She smiled at me, a tender, caring smile, her pale eyes sparkling. I basked in it. Laugh lines formed and her eyes widened. A plan was formulating in her head, I could tell.

"Was there a drugstore open when we came through town?" she asked.

At Perry Drugs, one of those massive stores that goes far beyond pharmaceuticals, she bought water-soluble K-Y lubricating jelly, Saran Wrap and surgical gloves.

"It's been three months — getting closer . . ." She let the possibilities hover. "But for now, we need surgical gloves — your hands are a mess from the fight," she said. "Let's see, for a drug store this place has all kinds of food. Do you prefer honey, chocolate syrup or strawberry jam?"

Honey sounded like the most unobtrusive choice to me. She chose the syrup.

I paid for the bagful of goodies, then had an idea of my own. At the A & P next door I picked up some apricot yogurt, a texture and aroma that I sensed would be a far better substitute than chocolate syrup.

"Well then, I think hollandaise sauce would be even better," Hayley laughed, picking up a tiny can. "And how about caviar?" In the deli section she found a small tin of a cheap variety.

"Ugh. Whatever turns you on. Anchovies maybe..." I aped a radio announcer's baritone: "You love 'em on pizza, now try 'em on pussy! Hey, come back here, I'm kidding!" I grabbed her sweatshirt and pulled her to me. Now *this* was foreplay.

Round mirrors in every corner of the store reminded me we were in the Midwest, and not Ann Arbor either. Blatant lesbianism probably wouldn't play in Imlay City. Reluctantly I let her go.

"How about Cool Whip?" I said.

"Marshmallow Creme!"

"Tapioca pudding!"

"Ben and Jerry's Rain Forest Crunch!"

"Enough!"

We left the store with the apricot yogurt and Cool Whip.

Back at the hotel, Hayley showed me how to spread the K-Y on her vulva and on the back of a double layer of plastic wrap, smooth the wrap on like a second skin, and then dribble on whatever tasty concoction I wanted, to camouflage the taste of the plastic.

Taking a shower in your raincoat? Not really. I soon forgot about any barrier and really got into it. It had been a long time.

This had become a real relationship, not a groupie thing. I was growing to love her. Though I couldn't imagine how in the world we could ever work out something long-range, she was willing to try. And so would I. I let my tongue tell her how much I cared.

It was my turn, and after the initial cool wetness of the K-Y, the jelly warmed and penetrated and I knew no difference between this lovemaking and the best I had ever experienced. Hayley knew how to tap out little patterns on my mons that brought back sensations that had retreated inside. In a low voice she talked to me of kaleidoscopes, of Pacific sunsets, of fields of wild flowers. My mind whirled with sensations that surfaced below.

I vowed to read the *Kama Sutra* again to see if anything from that straight love manual for the ages could be brought to my bed. I'd see if there were any new lesbian sex manuals at Sisterhood bookstore. Yes, when we got home I would try the ben wa balls, the dammits, the vibrators. For Hayley I would try anything.

Wake-up downer: we'd used every towel in the joint but still the bedsheets were a mess. I left extra tip money for the maid. Probably she'd seen worse.

I insisted Hayley have a full breakfast at the Big

Boy restaurant near the motel. Who knew what the day would bring?

We'd had a brief argument over what to wear. I'd insisted that we dress up a little since we'd be dealing with small-town authority figures, bound to be conservative.

"Laney, if you want to see women you think *must* be dykes, you need to look at the farm women you'll see," Hayley had insisted right back. "No makeup, short hair, flannel jackets, T-shirts, boots and jeans are the outfit of the day, even for going to town, for most of them."

"Sure, we're going to be mistaken for farmers," I said, rubbing my hands over her wispy curls. For the trip, she'd left behind the mustache wax that finally could turn her hair into a buzz. She really needed a trim for that style; her hair was an inch and a half now, adorable in her fluffy natural tendrils.

We compromised with ski sweaters, mine a blue snow scene, hers a gold turtleneck woven with fall leaves, worn over jeans and boots, perfect for the nippy Michigan October day. Fluffy banks of thick white clouds raced across an intense blue sky that rivaled the color of the Jeep Cherokee. The trees were ablaze. Hayley pointed out that the dried yellow crops were beans, the low green bushes were sugar beets, the sprawling vines hid winter squash. And everywhere was the corn, still drying for harvesting, miles upon miles of dense pale gold dried stalks.

"What's your plan of attack?" Hayley asked as we got into the car after walking Radar behind the restaurant.

"I thought we'd start at the newspaper and review old issues from nineteen fifty-nine, see if anything rings a bell there. Then we'll go by some of the places you remember in Bad Axe and end up at your home in Cadatunk. After that, we wing it," I admitted.

"Do you really think this will work?"

"I don't know. It depends on what else you've got buried in your memories, or on what other people remember. We'll see who else we can find to talk to."

In the sixty or so flat miles to Bad Axe there was one town of about twelve hundred, four mobile home sales lots, one mobile home factory, several hundred mobile homes on lots, several hundred farms, one McDonald's, one A & W Root Beer, and a half dozen restaurants all featuring the word *family*. "Home cooking," "country cooking," "breakfast specials" and "Fri–Sat nite buffet" appeared somewhere in their signs. I shuddered at the thought of lunch and dinner.

Fall colors were just past their prime, with perhaps a quarter of the leaves on the ground. The rest hung on in brilliant reds and golds against the blue sky, a sight that almost brought me to tears, remembering the seasons of my childhood. I forced myself to recall the Pacific. To think about driving these same roads on one of the winter days ahead when the temperature would hang around thirty-two degrees and sleet would coat the concrete and the bare tree limbs with ice.

The PI had already checked all the records in the county seat using his expertise; we weren't likely to find anything more in the government offices. The newspaper office referred us to the library for the microfilmed issues from that far back.

The small brick library was a block off the main street, next to a park that featured a restored log cabin village. "Saving our heritage," the park proclaimed. The whole town was a heritage park, from what I'd seen driving in. Stately homes — two with black-faced lawn jockeys amidst the shrubbery — proclaimed the small town of yore. I'd seen a faded "Get the U.S. Out of the U.N." sign in a field earlier that day.

"Can you imagine black-faced statues surviving the night in L.A.?" I said to Hayley.

"You're talking about Bad Axe, a town that last came to national attention when Richard Nixon was deciding whether to resign and he searched for the one place in the country which would still put on a parade welcoming him with loud applause."

I remembered that pathetic staged show of patriotism and loyalty. "That was Bad Axe?"

Hayley grinned. "It wasn't enough to save the bastard."

A few blocks out of town, mobile homes were the norm on small lots, while white farmhouses with porches on three sides and faded red barns, usually at a slant, anchored the hundred-acre holdings in between. So many barns, in such disrepair. They were eyesores, despite the public service ads back in L.A. begging for funds to restore "our national treasures." I wondered if the makers of those ads had any idea of the number and damage of these "treasures."

"Everybody builds pole barns now." Hayley pointed to structures shaped like a plain square house, but in sizes from glorified tool shed to factory. "They're cheaper and sturdier." Uglier, too.

While the main street of Bad Axe had such small, obviously historic stores as a family-owned bakery and a combination camera store and Christian bookstore, a new commercial strip just outside the city limits featured Wal-Mart, K mart, and all the usual fast-food chains. That was where the traffic was.

I could see the changing picture of rural America in this microcosm just as clearly as L.A.'s future was clear from an examination of Mount Washington. The county newspaper told the same tale: small department stores that had served farm families for fifty years were going bankrupt now that Wal-Mart *et al.* had arrived.

"None of this rings any bell," Hayley said as we pored over the microfilmed newspapers. In the entire year of 1959, there was definitely no mention of a murder or death resembling Hayley's memories of Len Hunsaker. Nothing in 1958 or 1960 either. We saw a news photograph of her singing "Silent Night" as a solo in the school Christmas pageant in 1958, her voice making her a standout even at that young age, but nothing more.

"Okay, we'll drive to your old home." I packed away the microfilm boxes and we left. Cadatunk was a few miles north.

"My God, the joint looks good!" Hayley exclaimed when she spotted the house she'd lived in. Somehow I'd pictured a tiny farmhouse with a rickety chicken coop in the rear. "They put on aluminum siding and they built a garage and addition," she said. "It really was a dinky place."

The chickens were gone, replaced by a substantial home garden that was still producing. The frost that had turned the leaves hadn't stopped these plants from mounding over with multi-colored hard-skinned winter squash and pumpkins like orange basketballs. Brussel sprouts by the hundreds tucked themselves under the leaves of other thick stalks. Potato plants indicated that the last of those harvests remained underground to be dug up. Acres of field corn spread to the right of the house, giving up the last of its moisture to the air, the better to survive storage when it was harvested. Yes, I could remember my own childhood, my own relatives' gardens not so very far from this part of Michigan.

She stared at the metallic cool lines of the house, the wealth of the garden. I got out of the car, Radar at my side.

A movement in the woods to the left of the house and behind the garden caught my attention. And Radar's. A young deer gave a flick of his white tail at us and ran for cover, Radar right behind.

"Radar!" I screamed. "Stop. Right now. That's an order. Stop! Get back here!"

My usually well-behaved shepherd was having none of it. She disappeared into the woods in hot pursuit. Hayley grabbed her purse and joined me in racing after the dog, to no avail. We stopped, panting, when we reached the woods and had no idea which way they had gone.

"Running a deer used to mean a fine of two thousand dollars and the dog gets shot on sight," Hayley said, watching my frustration.

"Radar! Stop! Come here!" I yelled over and over.

"It's October, probably archery season is on. Rifle

165

hunting won't be until November. The wardens don't pay too much attention to bow hunting, so she'll probably get away with it," Hayley tried to reassure me. "There's nothing you can do except wait until she gets exhausted and comes back to the car, tongue hanging, begging your forgiveness."

I could only hope she was right. We walked back to the car.

An elderly woman opened the front door of Hayley's old home. "May I help you, young ladies?" she asked.

"Oh, thank you. I used to live here a long time ago, and I was just admiring how much you'd done to the place," Hayley said.

"Oh, well then, you just have to see what it looks like inside too," the woman invited us. "I'm Mrs. Whiting, and I've got coffee perking and some marmalade muffins in the oven."

It was tempting. Hayley looked back at me. "Your choice," I whispered. "Ask how long she's lived here."

The woman had only moved in with her retired husband in 1991. She had no family in the area and had lived in Detroit before. She wouldn't know a thing about the Cadatunk of 1959.

"Do the Armstrongs still live across the street?" Hayley asked.

"Armstrongs? Oh, no, one of the big farm corporations owns all that land. Nobody's lived in that old house since I've been here."

"What about the rear barn?" Hayley questioned her.

"Umm, I don't know. I think maybe that it's still

in use for storage," Mrs. Whiting said. "I do recall seeing a hay baler loading something in there last year. Or was it the year before? I think the hay inside is all that's keeping it standing!"

Hayley and I looked at each other. Would we be able to go inside?

"Are you two young girls sure you don't want some lovely marmalade muffins? I've got an apple pie coming out of the oven in a half hour or so, if you can wait. Northern Spy apples off my own tree — very few Northern Spies left anymore. By the time we finish our muffins it'll be ready . . ."

"No, thanks again, I appreciate your offer, but there are some other places I want to see today, and I'm on a tight schedule," Hayley told her, matching her in politeness. She backed away, smiling and continuing to reassure the woman that it was all right, she didn't really have to see inside the house and have muffins and coffee, thanks again, yes the weather really had been lovely, no, she hadn't heard anything about a frost coming that night . . .

"She was desperate to have someone to talk to," I said. "Maybe we can come back later."

"Not if there's any way on earth I can avoid it," Hayley announced with finality. "Desperation scares me. Do you think you and I will ever get to desperate in our old age?"

"Not if there's any way on earth I can avoid it," I repeated her words. "I'm going to plant myself in the middle of a lesbian community somewhere and insist that they pay attention to their elders."

"Good luck — see how much attention young

lesbians pay to their elders in L.A. now," Hayley retorted. "How much the young and the old *anywhere* pay attention to each other."

We turned our attention across the street, to what remained of Armstrong Dairy.

CHAPTER SEVENTEEN

From the boarded-up windows and the way the tattered front door hung off its hinges, it was clear the main house was abandoned. Hayley stared intently at the field to the left of the farmhouse. "I think there should be something else there," Hayley whispered.

There was no need to whisper, unless she was also feeling as if we were at a funeral, or maybe a cemetery. We walked across the street, leaving the Cherokee in front of Hayley's old house, and attempted to walk up to the Armstrong home. The wooden porch creaked; I wouldn't chance putting it to the test of holding a person's weight anymore.

"All the electrical fence is down," Hayley noted. "The horses used to pasture over there, and the cows came home this way from the fields across the street." She motioned toward the fields of corn surrounding the Armstrong property. High as an elephant's eye, the show tune said, and it was.

"The cows crossed the main road every day?" I smiled at the picture of a Holstein-induced traffic jam.

"Morning *and* night," Hayley said.

"Are you getting any memories back?"

"No, just the one about the cows. Say, why did the cow cross the road?"

"Why?" I grimaced at the stupid joke that was coming.

"The chicken was on vacation."

I groaned aloud. Hayley laughed aloud, scanning the farm. She stopped suddenly.

"I see the rock pile where I buried the belt buckle!" Hayley yelled, running in that direction.

Her gold-patterned sweater swirled fall colors against the sky, repeating the trees. She was a leaf in flight. I jogged behind her. When I caught up she was on her knees, digging with her hands in the dirt and gravel.

"Help me move this monster," she said. We put our shoulders against the rock and tipped it over. Thick earthworms dug for cover in the exposed loamy black earth that smelled somehow of coffee grounds. "Now where is it?" Hayley muttered to herself, using a branch to move away more ground cover. She started to kick at the dirt with the heels of her Doc Martens. "*Where is it*!"

Her frantic groping worried me.

"HERE IT IS!" she screamed, dropping to the ground to get a closer look at the hunk of metal poking up through the stone pile. "IT'S REAL!"

"Uh huh." I took the buckle from her and wiped away the dirt. A stringy strand of leather trailed from the buckle, the last of the deteriorated belt. Turquoise stones, creased with dirt, surrounded the steer-horn design.

"That's it. I remembered right. I *did* kill Len Hunsaker," Hayley said over and over. She was going into some kind of self-induced anxiety state. I hugged her to me until she quieted down.

"Do you remember how?" I asked finally. She clinched her eyes tight and grimaced.

"No, nothing. Maybe we should go to the barn now."

I put the chunky buckle in my jacket pocket. We walked through weeds and remnants of a rutted path toward the faded gray wooden structure.

"Does it look strong enough to hold up?" I asked as she disappeared inside the double-wide door, large enough to drive a tractor through.

"Sure. The early farmers always made the barn the best and the house was an afterthought," Hayley said. "Despite what Mrs. Whiting said. Come on in."

The horses' stalls were filled with bales of hay. Though I'd seen mostly huge round bales drying in the fields as we'd driven up, these were old-fashioned, smaller rectangular bales.

"Here's the ladder," Hayley said quietly. I went to her side.

"Are you ready for this?" I asked, remembering how she wouldn't go up the ladder to my loft and now able to guess where that fear had come from.

Silently she pulled herself up the wooden rungs and disappeared through the hole in the ceiling to the second floor. A cloud of dust and straw stalks swirled down on me, tickling my nose, making me cough. Looking all around me for I knew not what, I followed her up through the hole. At the top I leaped to the side to land on soft loose hay and coarser straw. The air was warm and close, heavy with old broom smells.

Hayley had perched herself on a bale and was looking around her, lost in thought. I pulled up my own bale and sat across from her. I waited for Hayley to speak, to sort her way through what I hoped were fresh insights.

After a lengthy silence, she could only say, "I don't remember anything new."

My hopes fell. I had to reassure her, and in the process, myself. "Don't give up too soon," I said. "Maybe it will help to talk about the day your mother had her miscarriage. That's where you seem to be blocked."

Reluctantly she agreed.

"Okay, so after the priest left and I did my own baptism of the baby in the septic tank, I ran across the road to Armstrong Dairy," Hayley said, scrunching herself down into the hay. "First adult I came to was Mrs. Armstrong hanging clothes on the line, and she said she knew where my dad probably was and she'd drive one of the tractors to get him. Her oldest daughter, Lillian, would take care of the baby. The son, I think his name was Ritchie, was with his father someplace doing chores."

I watched her face as she strained to remember.

"We could hear the ambulance coming for my mother," Hayley went on, "and we ran out on their porch to see. Before I could even get to the road, the attendants had her out of her room and into their ambulance, and then they were gone. I went back inside the Armstrong house with Mrs. Armstrong." She couldn't speak for a while. Finally she continued: "I cried and cried, and Mrs. Armstrong said I should stay at her place until she got back from finding my father. She said I should pour myself some milk and watch television with her Lillian."

From the expression on her face I could tell she'd disliked Lillian.

"I remember, 'American Bandstand' was on, and I was too young to care about it. Lillian kept trying to get me to dance with her. She said I was no fun and then she ignored me. I went out into the kitchen and drank the milk and sat there for a while." Just as she sat silently for a while now. "I went back to my house and walked around in a daze. Patrick was fine, playing with his rabbits and chickens. I walked back to the Armstrong farm . . ." Hayley became silent again.

After a few minutes and no sign that she would finish her sentence, I urged her to continue. "What happened next, Hayley?"

"I remember now. Len was my friend. I went looking for Len."

"Who was Len?"

"He was a farmhand. He lived in a beat-up aluminum Airstream trailer home next to the Armstrong farmhouse. That's what I felt was missing a minute ago. And he was my only friend." She couldn't go on.

Finally she explained that Len came over to her one day when she was feeding apple cores to the Armstrong horses and wishing she could ride one of them.

"He introduced himself as the new farmhand, and then he picked out the gentlest mare and put me on her back and led me around for a while, holding on tight. I was seven, and I was in love, with horses and with Len."

For the next two years, Len spent a lot of time with her, though she remembered that he had to hide from Mr. Armstrong to do it.

"He was always goofing off, just daring Mr. Armstrong to fire him, but I guess help was hard to find so he got along." She gasped. "And he always had a bottle of cherry wine from the Armstrongs' basement!"

I snapped to attention.

"Mr. Armstrong made wine every year from some of the cherry trees in their orchard, and he was really proud of it. He gave away lots of it, even tried to give my dad a bottle, but Dad felt that the Armstrongs were too rich, too snobbish. I guess they did have a kind of paternalistic attitude toward people with less money than they had."

She put her nose up in the air in unconscious imitation.

"They treated Len like shit, so I thought he was

really smart to get back at them by hiding out and drinking their wine. I remember Mr. Armstrong did take some tips from Len on how to improve the wine because Len had worked in a winery someplace."

The one the private investigator had found. Hayley talked about how she and Len would hide up in the hayloft of the horse barn, when he was supposed to be at the milking barn or out in the fields.

"If Mr. Armstrong ever did come into that building looking for him, we'd duck into the grain bins." She laughed at the memory. "You had to watch it when the bins were totally full because you could suffocate in the grain. But it was great most of the year."

She laughed to herself. "I loved the feel of oats. They shifted around under you real good, and they were kind of soft. Even though you look at an oat and it's hard and pointy and polished, when you lay down in a bunch of them it's like being on a great mattress."

She spread her hands over the hay as if to transform it into a huge mattress of oats. "One day we were up in the hayloft, drinking wine and giggling over something, when he said he had to pee. I figured he'd hike over to the outhouse by his trailer. The Armstrongs had indoor plumbing and so did we, but Len was supposed to use the outhouse except for his Saturday night bath in their house."

One of the relatives I'd stayed with in the early fifties had had an outhouse. My nose involuntarily wrinkled at my own memories of fighting off huge white hissing geese, blocking my path to their outhouse with flailing wings on winter mornings. Hayley didn't notice.

"He didn't want to take the chance of being seen, so he looked out the window where the hay baler sends the bales into the second story loft along a kind of conveyor belt. There it is!" Hayley pointed to a place in the wall where different colors of faded wood showed that a window had been boarded over from the outside. "When he didn't see anybody, he pulled out his thing and peed out the window in a big arc, two stories high. The pee really splattered and kicked up dust when it hit the ground."

I could picture the scene.

"I laughed and then I tried it and of course ended up dribbling all over myself. He helped me wipe off with hay, and then he asked me if I'd touch him for a little while." Hayley's smile ended. "And from then on, whenever we hung out, I'd hold his penis in my hands and stroke it, and he'd put his hand down there on me and we'd just touch each other. It was real comforting."

I didn't like hearing this part.

Hayley kept on. "I read somewhere that in some primitive cultures, mothers play with their babies' genitals to get them to stop crying or go to sleep. Whenever I felt keyed up from Mom acting funny, or from Dad worrying about money, or Patrick getting on my nerves, I'd hunt down Len and see if he could get away for a while. And I think he did the same with me."

I shuddered as she talked.

"It didn't feel bad or nothing, but I guess I knew that the other adults wouldn't understand so we hid pretty good. This didn't happen a lot, mainly during the summer when I was out of school, but a little bit the rest of the year when it wasn't real cold out. He said he was my boyfriend and he was going to wait until I grew up and could get married. I felt really special and grown up."

She had a smile on her face, remembering. The smile made me feel sick.

"What happened the day your mom had the miscarriage? Did you go find Len then?"

Her entire body did an involuntary jerk.

"I saw him with Mr. Armstrong and I guess Len could tell from my face that I needed to see him. He made a motion toward our barn and I knew to go up and wait for him, that he'd get away as soon as he could." Her voice was very quiet. "I was always nervous climbing the ladder and making the swing through the hole and onto the floor of the loft without someone there to catch me if I slipped. But I did it, and I settled down in the hay and waited for Len." She was quiet again.

"Did he ever show up?"

"Oh, sure, in ten or fifteen minutes. He had some wine, and we both drank a lot. I was crying, I remember, and I told him the whole miserable story. He comforted me and told me how beautiful I was and how he was going to marry me when I grew up because I was such a wonderful girl and had suffered so much, just like him, and we were kindred souls destined for each other. Words to that effect." She grimaced at the memory.

"He undid my blouse and rubbed my chest and played with my nipples. He did that too sometimes. Titties, he called them, and he said they were going to be real big one day, he could tell. He was right about that one." She sniffled. "He kept touching my nipples and it felt good, and he said he could tell they were getting bigger already just by his playing with them. He had me play with his penis and he took off all my clothes. He kissed me, which he'd only done once or twice before, but this time he kept on kissing me. And then he lay on top of me. His penis was touching me down there, kind of twitching against me. It felt good, I have to tell you. Somebody loved me. Plus I liked the feelings inside. I'd had at least half the bottle of wine."

Cherry wine, I was sure.

"I began to feel that we shouldn't be doing this, that it shouldn't be feeling this good, that there was something wrong with me that this should feel so good, that it was my fault that I was doing this thing that probably shouldn't be feeling so good." Her voice raced as her thoughts became circular. "But as long as Len was holding me, I wasn't thinking about my mom and whether she would die and leave me all alone, and whether I'd sent the baby to limbo and committed some horrible sin. Being with Len felt like less of a sin. I led him on. I know I did."

I had to interrupt that line of self-blame. "It wasn't your fault, Hayley. You were nine years old. Your body couldn't handle the adult situation." I was frozen in place, wanting to be next to her, not sure that I should be. Touching her now would somehow pull me into her tragedy, I felt. And pull her out of it. She needed to relive it more than she needed to be comforted. I forced myself to hold back, to give my sympathy with words.

"So finally he let out something like a groan and got up on his knees and yanked his pants down and spread my legs and entered me. I couldn't believe what he was doing. I wasn't even sure *what* he was doing. It hurt like hell, and it jolted me awake from my dream world where my best friend was keeping my problems at bay."

I wanted to kill this Len. And half the men in the world.

Her story was not over. "I made some noise and he put his hand over my mouth and told me it would only hurt for a minute and it was going to feel real good in just a few seconds. So I shut up and waited for it to feel good. I guess I still wanted to believe him."

My own thoughts were going round and round, seeking an out.

"He kept pushing into me so hard my whole body kept shifting all over the hayloft. We weren't in the oats bin, we were on hard stalks of hay that ripped into my back and my legs and scratched me all over. He wouldn't stop, he didn't care, he didn't notice. I think that's what hurt the most. He just kept ripping into me, and then he came and collapsed on top of me like a deadweight." Her body slipped in her seat as if a weight had just hit her now. "He lay there for what seemed like hours, not moving. I bounced my body around some to try to shift him off of me, and that got him going again. 'Hey, you *like* it!' he said to me. 'You want some more, hey? I told you it'd feel good.'"

My stomach churned.

"And he went at it again, saying things to me like he loved me and this meant we were engaged and we'd be married someday when I got old enough and we'd keep doing this over and over for the rest of our lives and didn't it feel good, honey and all that kind of shit. What's worse, by then it did feel kind of good, if I didn't think about how my underside was being scratched all up. The fact that I could feel something enjoyable through all this convinced me that I did deserve it, I must want it."

"You were nine years old," I reminded Hayley. "Even little kids have sexual feelings. Parts of our bodies work on automatic. Rape victims sometimes have orgasm but it's still rape. It wasn't your fault." I could tell she wasn't hearing me. She waved my interruption away and kept going.

"This time when he came he really collapsed, out cold. He'd chug-a-lugged half the bottle too. My circulation had stopped in both my legs and I kept getting angrier and angrier at him for ruining what I'd thought was a friendship. I'd needed him and he hadn't done what I needed. I wasn't sure what had happened but I knew this was really, really wrong. He'd gone over some line or other, and I was just as much to blame as he was because I hadn't stopped him at any point."

She wouldn't hear my argument, I knew.

"And I was getting scared, scared of being caught this time with no clothes on and scared of what was going on with my mom and scared that I should be back home. I was mad at him for not moving." Her voice was getting quiet again. "So with all my strength I whipped myself up and pushed him off. We hadn't noticed how close we'd gotten to the hole in the loft floor by the ladder.

"He fell down the hole!

"He didn't even scream or say a word. His arms and legs were going in all directions, trying to hold onto something, anything. You've heard of grasping for straws? Literally, that's all he could grab."

She flashed a crooked, taut grimace of a smile.

"He just let out a couple of groans, and there were some shifting sounds and it didn't sound like I thought it would, like if he'd landed on the concrete floor. Then there was no sound at all." Just as she didn't say anything for a few minutes. "I was so scared I peed into the hay as I lay there. Finally I got up enough courage to crawl over to the edge of the hole and there he was — impaled on a pitchfork."

I gasped at the image, my throat closing.

"He had five big old steel spikes coming right through his body in different places, one of them through his neck, one through his brain, the rest through his chest."

"A pitchfork," I said. "Five prongs, like the tool used on me in the shower."

She nodded in horrified recognition, and continued. "The pitchfork had to have been standing up against the wall by the ladder where somebody left it, and Len had kicked it loose as he fell or something. He was hanging in midair where the pitchfork and his body were caught against the wall. Anyway, Len was dead, no question about it. Even at nine years old, I knew that."

Involuntarily I remembered seeing my dead grandmother in her casket when I was about nine and knowing she was dead, even though she looked so lifelike.

Hayley continued in her barely audible voice. "And there I was. I got dressed fast, all the while trying to figure out what to do. I figured my only chance was to make it look like an accident, like Len had been up in the hayloft drinking when he lost his footing and fell and kicked the pitchfork loose. It was the truth, only without my part in it."

She'd been a quick thinker for a little girl, I noted to myself.

"I made sure the wine bottle was out in the open and I put fresh hay over where I'd peed — if they could smell it when they found Len they'd probably just think he'd peed in the loft, since men'll pee anywhere."

She looked at me for my smile. I forced one.

"I climbed around him and got down on the floor, where his blood was turning the straw maroon and making little rivers of red-tinged chaff on the concrete that I had to avoid smearing. I had to work fast before the blood spread anymore. I pulled his underpants up and tugged his jeans on as best I could. I remember how hard it was to do up those brass buttons on his fly."

With a chill I remembered seeing Hayley's rapist in June buttoning, not zipping, his fly.

"I couldn't figure out how to do his belt buckle — it had a silver long-horned steer with turquoise accents on it — so I took off his belt all together and tucked it in my waistband. I had on black jeans and a homemade flour-sack blouse myself, I remember."

I too had worn those shirts made from flour and feed sacks by my father's sisters. The image slid out of my mind as I was brought back to Hayley's story.

"I saw some horse manure and got the idea to put some on his boots and some on the rungs of the ladder so it would look like he'd slipped. He had on red shoelaces and I remember laughing aloud like a maniac at the funny sight and then looking around again to make sure no one heard me. I picked up that fresh manure in my left hand and smeared it along the ladder till it looked right and then I was stuck with this filthy hand."

Brave kid, I thought.

"I swished it around in the horse trough and wiped it off on some straw from the floor. I remember shaking all over and hating how my hand smelled, hating how I smelled, hating what had happened, hating Len."

I was sure I hated Len this moment as much as she ever had.

"Before I left the barn I looked around very carefully to make sure nobody would see me, and I scooted out and over to the horse pasture. Everybody knew I went there a lot, so nothing would be suspicious if I was spotted there. I saw this big pile of rocks and boulders that the Armstrongs had pulled out of their fields and dumped in one place, and it hit me that this would be a good place to bury the belt because nobody would ever move those rocks. I tucked the belt and the buckle in behind one of the biggest stones and piled lots of dirt on it to make sure."

I touched the buckle now resting in my pocket.

"Nobody had seen me at all, I was pretty sure. So I went home and washed my hands really good with my dad's Lava soap and the Fels Naptha both. I washed down there too. My legs were a mess, all scratched up from the hay, but I could cover that by saying I fell. I put on clean long-legged jeans and socks to go with my red leather sandals."

I remembered the sturdy red leather sandals all little girls wore in those days, with the punched out design across the toes.

"I made it just in time, because about then Dad came back and got me and Patrick and took us in his truck down to the hospital. He told Patrick she had a bad cold. 'Mommy didn't have a cold this morning,' Patrick said. He always was a bright kid. But everybody lies to kids. Dad looked at me like he knew I knew how sick she was, but he didn't say anything."

The scene was a repeat of many I'd experienced in my own childhood.

"Me and Patrick had to stay in the lobby while he went up to see her," Hayley said. "We had to wait a long, long time, and then he came down and said she was all right, but she was going to have to stay in the hospital a few days, and he was going to take us to his mother's house till Mom could come home. We went back to our house and I kept looking to see when the police would get to the Armstrongs' but nobody came."

I couldn't figure out why, either.

"Dad grabbed a bunch of our clothes and drove us to Bay City where his folks lived, and when Mom got out of that hospital she had to go to another one in Caro, I think for her depression, so Patrick and I were at Grandma's for the rest of the summer. When Dad came to get us, he drove us to our new home in Saginaw, and we never went back to Cadatunk."

Her body eased down into the hay even more. The end. Only it wasn't.

"You never heard what happened to Len and the Armstrongs?"

"Never a word. For years I kept looking over my shoulder, sure the cops were going to take me away to jail. I remember now that I even tried to confess that I'd murdered somebody, but the priest didn't believe me. That was the beginning of the end of my faith. Actually it had probably died when the Bad Axe priest accused me of dooming that fetus to limbo for all eternity."

"And I thought I had good reason to be out of the church," I murmured. We were both quiet for a while.

"So that's *your* story, you lying bitch!" a male voice on the ground floor of the barn shouted up at us.

CHAPTER EIGHTEEN

The voice boomed, "Now you're going to hear the *truth* !"

Shocked, Hayley and I clung to each other.

"Len!" she shouted.

"No, not Len, you stupid cunt," the voice said. "Look at me."

Trembling, we leaned forward and looked down the hole. There was the man who'd slashed me with the garden tool, who'd raped Hayley in the alley months before, wearing his uniform of white T-shirt, button-fly jeans, red-laced sneakers and belt buckle of silver and turquoise. Hay chaff like dandruff lay on top of his brown crew-cut and wiry shoulders. He posed with a pitchfork the jaunty way Fred Astaire would lean on his dancing cane.

But then the dim light gleamed against his crazed eyes and I saw instead the face of Rumpelstiltskin. I remembered the fairy tale of the gnome taunting the miller's daughter when she couldn't guess his name, dancing in rage when she finally spoke the name aloud until he broke through the floor and disappeared in a whirlwind frenzy.

I looked at Hayley, who stared at the man through narrowed eyelids. Her turtleneck seemed to choke her white face off from her body.

"You're Len," she said again.

"No, no, you killed Len. Didn't you just find his belt buckle where you buried it? Think again . . ."

Hayley screwed up her face, as if she could make him disappear by wishing hard. But the man did not go away. I couldn't shake the comparison to Rumpelstiltskin: he danced a taunting jig while Hayley struggled with his identity.

"I watched you that day, you know. I watched you every day. I watched you and Len every time you got together. I watched and I listened, and I saw every time you stole him away from me."

His lined, tanned face contorted with emotion as he spat every syllable with obvious hate aimed at Hayley. He jabbed up at us with the pitchfork.

Hayley glanced at me quickly. "I don't know who he is," she whispered.

"Oh, yes, you do, Hayley," the man said, twirling the pitchfork like a baton. "Remember the boy who played doctor with you the summer you first moved to Cadatunk, before you started school in the fall? I was just five years old, and you did everything I asked you to." He hissed the last words.

I grabbed for Hayley's hand and squeezed tight.

"Ritchie?" Hayley whispered.

"That's right, you finally got it right," the man said. "Ritchie Armstrong." His voice mocked the childlike intonation, the deranged imitation of what he must have intended to be Hayley's young voice.

"Ritchie!" Hayley said again, sitting back on her feet. "I never thought of you."

Helplessly I wished for Max's gun, still locked in the trunk of the Jeep.

"That's right, you never thought of me," the man jeered. "You were even more curious than me, remember?"

"Now I do," Hayley said, barely breathing.

"You were seven and I was five, and I thought you were the most beautiful girl in the entire world and I told you I was going to marry you when I grew up and you *laughed* at me. But who's laughing now?" His voice was a cackle. "Do you remember that too?" His voice rose like a singer doing scales, the jabbing pitchfork accenting each word like a conductor's baton.

"No," Hayley whispered.

"Speak up. Did you say no? Of course you said no. But you never said no. Not to Len. Once Len got here, you never remembered me again. I was just some flyspeck on the wall, and you spent all your time with Len. What you didn't know is that he also spent his time with ME!"

The voice shouted out the last word. Hayley

recoiled. I held on tight, feeling her ribcage heave under her sweater.

Ritchie spewed out a line of hatred for Hayley, for Len, for life itself. It was hard to follow. The essence seemed to be that Len had also promised Ritchie that they would always be together. Ritchie hid out in the barley bin whenever Len and Hayley were together, listening to the two of them.

"Did Len know?" Hayley barely breathed the words.

"Say what, bitch? Louder!"

"Did Len know?"

"Of *course* he knew. He told me to do it! We always had our own fun after you left. Better'n yours." Ritchie drew close to us, his foot on the first rung of the ladder. We retreated as far as we could and still watch what he was doing.

I looked around for anything that could be a weapon. All I could do was shove down one of the hay bales if he tried to come up the ladder at us. But he stayed on the ground floor. I asked him what happened that last day. He refused to talk to me. Hayley repeated my question and he continued in a taunting way, feeding out bits and pieces of information, watching our reactions.

"The last day I didn't get here fast enough. I was stuck down here listening, just like I am now. I was holding a pitchfork just like this." He paused again. His look at Hayley overflowed with hatred. "Bet you'd like to know the rest of what happened that last day, wouldn't you?"

She nodded silently.

"I can't hear you." We could see his head below,

his blue eyes bulging. His jawline jutted forward so much his entire face was distorted. He jumped back from the ladder and paced in tight circles, clutching the pitchfork like a lifeline.

"Tell me what happened!" Hayley said aloud, her fear making her voice high-pitched.

"Don't mind if I do," the man said with a satisfied leer. "In due time. You got it all wrong, you know."

He proceeded to tell us how he hid in the linen closet of Kitt's house and heard Hayley tell me her life story. I was sure I'd checked that closet, but apparently not thoroughly enough, not behind the vacuum cleaner and bags of old clothes waiting to be taken to Goodwill.

He'd gotten a full set of keys on a day when we'd gone out and left one deadbolt unlocked. He was living in the basement of the abandoned hotel next to Kitt's, hiding his inconspicuous white Ford Escort a few blocks away, moving it every few days.

"You're so goddamned predictable," he sneered at Hayley. "I knew you'd go back to Betty Ford after I got you in the alley last June . . . oh, yes, I've had you plenty in my life."

Hayley shuddered in my arms.

"I even moved into the commune in Oregon to be with you, and I fucked you anytime I wanted. You couldn't get enough those days. You never did recognize me."

Hayley screwed up her face. "I can't place him there," she muttered to me.

"Damn right you can't. I had a beard and long

hair then. You used to look good. You look ugly bald."

"Start from the beginning," Hayley begged. "I can't follow all you're saying."

"*I can't follow all you're saying,*" the man mocked Hayley in a singsong. "You haven't been able to figure anything out since I met you."

He put aside the pitchfork and sat down on his own bale of hay on the first floor, looking up at our two faces through the ladder hole. Hayley and I shifted in place so that we were crouched on the straw looking down at Ritchie.

"The day your mom had that miscarriage, I was listening to you tell my mom about it. When Lillian tried to get you to dance to 'American Bandstand' with her" — Ritchie jumped up and did something that must have been intended as the Twist — "I was listening in the next room." Self-satisfied, he sat back down again and continued. "When you went out to find Len and then went to the hayloft and waited for him, I listened to both of you from below." He shook his head in disgust. "Anyway, I was standing right about here, and I was holding a pitchfork just like this one, right about here," Ritchie said, getting up and finding the right position. "I was just *standing* here, you understand, and all of a sudden Len's body is *flying* through the air and landing *right on my pitchfork!*" He screamed the last words, his head thrown back, his eyes squeezed tight.

We were all silent for a moment, stunned by his outburst and the image.

"Len was bleeding all over me and his legs were

draped all over me. I couldn't hold the pitchfork up; it fell over against the wall and I got the hell out of there. I wanted to run away, but I stuck around long enough to see *you* do your cleanup and bury the belt buckle."

"What happened to the body?" Hayley asked.

Finally he seemed less sure of himself. For a moment I could see the connection between this demented fool and the little boy who had too much happen to him. I calculated that he'd been only seven years old.

"I, ah, told my father what happened."

"*Everything?*" Hayley shouted. "Why didn't the police come get me like I thought they would?" I held her tightly as her whole body quivered.

"Yeah, just about everything. 'Course I blamed you for most of it, but he didn't believe me. He kept saying it was all *my* fault. He said I'd made up the part about you. It didn't help when Lillian lied and said you'd been with her all afternoon while Mom was gone."

"So that's why he didn't believe you," Hayley said, her body clinging against mine.

Ritchie didn't hear her. "Lillian didn't want to get in trouble for letting you slip away. Dad didn't tell her why he wanted to know your whereabouts. He never told Mom neither."

From his jumbled words that followed, we decoded that Ritchie had helped his father hide the body in the barn for the rest of that day. In the middle of the night his father got up and dug a hole for Len and buried him near where the belt buckle was buried, also figuring that nobody would ever dig up anything under the rock pile.

Hayley and I looked at each other. He caught our glances.

"Oh, yeah, it's still there. Only you're never gonna get a chance to have it dug up. My dad didn't believe everything was your fault. He blamed me. He said I was crazy." Ritchie let out a long, exaggerated sigh like an actor playing to the balcony. "He never turned me in to the police, but his farming days were over. The sign over the dairy used to say, 'Armstrong and Son.' He had it painted out and sold the farm. We used to be friends — he used to take me fishing and hunting and stuff — but he never did anything with me again. You took my daddy away from me too."

It seemed important to keep him talking. When he fell silent, as he had now, I could almost see the demons whirring by his ears as he fidgeted and talked to himself and maybe unseen others, forty years of memories hurtling through his head.

As we watched, the little-boy look dissipated. The ghost-stalker was back. He stood up straight and looked around him as if wondering where he was.

"What did your father do afterward?" Hayley asked, her voice coaxing back the human little boy.

"Huh?" It took a minute for him to realize that a question had been asked. He looked up to the hayloft and beamed a beatific smile that turned demoniac when his tongue rolled forward like a bulky slug crawling on his lower lip.

Hayley repeated herself.

He shook his head like a dog worrying a bone as he spoke. "The bastard moved to Flint. Got a job at GM. Retired to Florida."

Hayley asked him how he made a living. From

his ramblings, we figured out that he'd worked odd jobs on other farms, sometimes he'd pumped gas, sometimes he'd worked for quick-lube shops in L.A.

"You were getting famous and I was getting nothing. You had lots of money and I was always broke. Everywhere I worked, there was your voice shouting at me on the radio." He paused. "I'm a veteran, you know. The first few years you were in that lunatic place in Oakland, I was in 'Nam. But even there I couldn't escape hearing you on the radio all the time, even in the jungle."

I couldn't believe the military had taken him, but they were pretty desperate in the early seventies.

"You knew I was in Synanon?" Hayley looked ashen.

"I knew every time you farted. First time I heard you sing that song on the radio with that nigger, I knew it was you. I left school and hitchhiked to L.A. the next year when you started doing those concerts."

"And you started sending me the wine." Hayley sank into my arms even more tightly. His eyes narrowed when he saw me hug her more closely.

"Cunt-suckers," he said, barely aloud, then remembered Hayley's last question. "You betcha. I used some of my dad's stuff for a while. It seemed only right after the way Len poured it down your gullet. Then I picked up cherry wine anyplace I could. But I got it to you before every concert. I'd pay some kid a buck to deliver it."

His triumphant grin made my hair rise on the back of my neck.

"How'd you keep track of me all those years?"

"Oh, you were in the papers a lot. I just followed you. I'm not stupid."

"Why'd you do it, Ritchie?" Hayley's voice was plaintive.

"Why? Why not? You ruined my life. It was the least I could do to return the favor. It got to be kind of fun, driving you crazy every way I could."

I stroked Hayley's forehead and her damp, fine short hair. Her breathing came in quick pants.

"It's all your fault," Ritchie ranted. "You're the one who pushed Len down the ladder. *Somebody* had to punish you."

"Why didn't you just kill me?"

"Hey, and end all the fun? I was having a good time making you suffer, bitch. Didn't I do a good job?"

She refused to look at him.

"Ask him if he intended to kill you in the shower," I whispered to Hayley. She repeated the question aloud.

"Hell, no. Tell your dyke friend that *she* was the real target. I just wanted *you* to think *you'd* killed her, is all. A bottle of wine down you and you wouldn't know what happened."

Hayley was shaking in my arms.

"I wanted her out of the way, but I didn't figure how strong she was. Should'a bought some chloroform or ether before I took her on." He did his little dance to unheard music.

"Ask him how he knew to find us here," I said in my lowest voice. She did.

"Like I said, you're so predictable," Ritchie said with a faked yawn. "Even though you got smart when you hooked up with that bitch. I need to thank you, Laney, for buying a car that's so easy to track. I knew some day you'd figure out enough to make you come back here. Right to this very barn."

I looked over at Hayley. She was the fainting goat again. Of all the times. Ritchie droned on.

"I've been waiting for you a couple of hours, knowing this was the day. The big day. Game's over. You're no fun anymore."

These last words made me more frightened. Did he have a gun? If he came at us with only the pitchfork we had a good chance. "You'll get caught this time, Ritchie," I said. "You got sloppy. Why don't we all just talk things out some more?"

He'd already disappeared from view, muttering and humming to himself. I heard a sound like the pitchfork clattering against concrete. A liquid sloshing out of a can.

Suddenly I smelled a wispy trace of kerosene. Then smoke.

I froze. Fire! In a dry barn full of instantly combustible straw and hay, we'd explode like a Christmas tree in May. In panic I looked down at the first floor. It was already consumed in fire, crackling flames racing up the rough-hewn wood walls in a whoosh, spewing embers every which way that erupted into thousands of new fires, soon to be caught into one monstrous blaze.

The first fiery tendril crawled up the ladder toward me. Black smoke rolled into the second floor, grabbing air right out of my throat. I saw no way out.

CHAPTER NINETEEN

Hayley's nose twitched; she came to life.

"Ram it, right there!" Hayley yelled, pointing at the boarded-over window she'd noticed earlier. We grabbed each other around the waist and in unison battered the wall with our shoulders and backs with all our might until we beat the boards loose. The creaking planks flapped in the air, their short rusty nails pointing at us like talon-tipped tiger paws. Flames licked our feet.

"Jump!" I screamed, and we leaped with all our strength. We were flying through the air, broken wood and nails ripping at our clothes, heated air whooshing at our skin, smoke rasping into our lungs.

And then we were hitting the patch of high weeds behind the barn and rolling over and over in the rasping tangle of grass and brambles and loamy dirt underneath the brush.

I lay still for a precious second, pain sluicing through my body. I felt for torn stitches, moving each leg and arm to make sure they worked, coughing out the smoke. Hayley did the same. We were both all right. The wall of heat reached for us, enveloped us. We rolled more and scrambled to our feet and took off like cheetahs toward the field of yellowed corn stalks, tall enough to hide an elephant, and disappeared into the maze.

I tried to see Ritchie as we ran but he was nowhere in sight. Hopefully he was confident we were dying in the fire. I'd feel more in control if I knew where he was.

"We'd better find Ritchie before he finds us," I yelled. We kept our heads down and fought our way through the dried cornstalks back toward the entrance of the barn.

We moved through the closely packed tall corn plants like moles digging a tunnel, trying not to make visible ripples on the surface above us. When we figured we were in view of the barn entrance we crept to the edge of the corn and looked out through the straggly stalks.

"Radar!" I yelled.

Ears up, the white shepherd looked over at me in doggie delight, then back at her cornered prey. Ears down. Ritchie danced in the door of the burning barn, screaming at Radar to get away, to let him go.

Radar did a dance herself, turning toward Hayley and me in obvious desire to come say hello and probably beg forgiveness, then lunging back at Ritchie, fangs bared, her growls and snarls keeping him trapped in the flaming archway.

The burning support beam over the door gave way with a thunder-crack and plummeted onto Ritchie's back, spiking him to the ground. Radar leapt back. Flames raced off of the beam and up and down the length of Ritchie's body. His arms and legs jerked and twitched and his head rolled, his thin wail ripping the air, piercing my eardrums. I jammed my hands against my ears and tried to keep out the prolonged howl that I knew would stay with me all of my life, haunting me in my nightmares and in dark moments of the days.

The scream gurgled and died.

"Wait!" I grabbed at Hayley's sweater to stop her from running toward the body. "That whole roof's going to go."

The molten barn gave way as I spoke, collapsing in one motion, flames shooting fifty feet in the air. A white-hot aura flooded the sky. Radar huddled in my arms in palpable terror. The three of us clung together as waves of heat rushed over us.

For a second I was terrified that the flames would spread in our direction, but I felt the dampness of the dirt beneath us, the succulent green grass and weeds between us and the fire.

We cuddled in a relieved heap, Radar licking our faces, Hayley kissing my cheeks, our embrace tossing all of us to the ground where we tumbled around in a hug of gratitude.

When the flames died down enough to approach the barn, we walked with dread toward the place where we had last seen Ritchie. The wall of heat, shimmering like a mirage, kept us from getting close.

A flash of white gristle in the ashes caught my eye. "There he is," I said.

All that could be seen in the rubble was Ritchie's hand, fingers charred black in a claw, with graying ashes flaking away in the breezes kicked up by the smoldering fire. A thin layer of meaty red flesh and bands of white cartilage showed beneath the char at the palm where burned skin peeled back from white bone. Blood and clear liquid oozed from the blackened flesh, puddling in the ashes underneath and evaporating in steam.

Hayley gagged. I turned away. Radar whimpered and tried to approach but the heat pushed her back. She retreated to my side.

A siren wailed somewhere, the sound coming closer. Mrs. Whiting must have called the fire department. The chartreuse yellow fire truck pulled up the driveway and kept on driving over the weeds to get as close as possible to the barn. A half-dozen men, in various stages of fire-fighting attire, scrambled off the truck.

"They're volunteers," Hayley whispered.

Several pickups were pulling in behind the truck, more volunteers piling onto the scene.

"There's a body there." I pointed as two men unwound a hose and aimed it toward the barn. The bulk of the fire truck was a water tank. They stopped and looked quizzically where I directed, then called another man over. He stared at the hand, then approached Hayley and me. Radar growled and I tapped her nose.

"What happened here?" he asked.

The rest of the fire fighters kept the high-pressure hose away from the area of Ritchie's body as they drenched the last embers. Another man talked into a radio and soon more sirens could be heard in the distance. Mrs. Whiting stood on her front porch across the street, watching. Kids were running down the road from all directions toward the fire. More cars pulled up alongside the highway and their passengers joined the flow of sightseers coming our way.

CHAPTER TWENTY

We told the highlights of the story to the fire department captain, and he called in the county sheriff. We told him the entire story. He sat there with pencil and paper, dumbfounded, as if unsure how much to put down.

A high-school student who was the son of the owner of a local radio station came by the sheriff's office in Bad Axe to check on the fire. He asked a few questions, obviously having no idea what he was doing or what was going on.

"Two women from California, Laney Samms and

Hayley Malone, who were visiting Bad Axe today were present when a fire destroyed a barn at the abandoned Armstrong Dairy farm," his radio news report said. "It is unconfirmed that a former Cadatunk resident was burned to death in the fire. The sheriff's office is investigating." The fire chief was quoted on the size of the fire, the estimated value of the barn and contents, and the number of barn fires in Huron County so far this year.

That was the total story. The sheriff shared a wry smile with us as we listened to the radio in his office. A few minutes later the phone rang.

"Yes, it's that Hayley Malone," he told the caller. "I'm sorry. It's my job," he told us. "That was the reporter's father — he made the connection. He went to school with you, Hayley. I'm afraid things are going to get very hot for you. But we're going to need you to stick around a few days for more questions if you can."

Hayley excused herself to make phone calls to her brother and to her father. "I don't want them to hear about this from anyone else," she explained. She was gone a long time. Tear-tracks lined her sooty cheeks when she returned.

Two hours later an Associated Press reporter from Detroit arrived on the scene and took charge of getting a more complete story out on the wire service to all media. I excused myself and called Kitt to tell her what had happened and to get some advice on how to handle what probably would be a flood of media requests. "Say as little as possible, and we'll talk more about this tonight," Kitt said.

The police found Len's body where we said it would be, and eventually they recovered what was left of Ritchie. We told them that Ritchie's father had retired to Florida and a few calls found his parents, who were notified by Florida state police. Dental records later proved the body was indeed Richard Armstrong, Jr.

Hayley gave bare-bones interviews to the first wave of media. We holed up in a motel the first night and Hayley and Kitt argued on the phone over which media to give any exclusives to and which to shine on.

Hayley felt she owed a favor to a woman who'd done a favorable interview of her for *Rolling Stone* years ago, at a time when she wasn't being treated well in the press. The woman now worked for *Vanity Fair,* and Kitt arranged for her to get the most complete story.

Reporters' phone calls to our motel room awoke us at dawn, and both reporters and photographers were camped outside our door when we tried to go out for breakfast. I called Kitt again; through her connections she tracked down a lesbian attorney who lived in nearby Caseville, who came and got us and hid us at her home on Lake Huron. We left a message at the sheriff's office that we would come down twice a day for interviews in their conference room, but they were not to tell anyone where we were staying.

Our host also put up the *Vanity Fair* reporter who arrived later that day, on the heels of *People, Newsweek, Time, Entertainment Weekly, Us* and a dozen other national media. The *Vanity Fair* reporter stayed with us for two full days and took hundreds of photos as well as three notepads full of notes. The other reporters and photographers camped out at the sheriff's office waiting for our twice-daily appearances. We took winding back roads to Caseville to avoid being followed. Mrs. Whiting was interviewed so often she left town to stay with her sister.

That was our life for more than a week. *People* did the nicest of the quickie stories, even hinting I was more than just a friend, the role the rest of the media assigned to me.

I let Hayley take the lead in determining how "out" she wanted to be, considering that she might want to use this publicity to finally attempt a comeback. "Everybody knows I'm a drunk and an addict and a sex fiend and a has-been," she said to me. "They never really pinned the label lesbian on me. Like Janis, I loved everybody and everything. So they know but they don't know. And I don't know how hard I want to push the lesbian issue right away, on top of everything else."

Only to her friend at *Vanity Fair* did she open up completely, and even then she told the reporter that she'd prefer that her sexual orientation be downplayed. That story wouldn't come out for several months, however. Meanwhile the media had a field day with Hayley's story. Hayley and her "friend."

That was all we were that week, actually, with all of its tensions and demands. Hayley was understandably upset, shaken to her roots by finding out what had happened to her life. Bundled in sweaters, she spent much of the time walking alone on the Lake Huron shore.

It came time to leave, and I packed my suitcase

and said my good-byes to our Caseville host. Hayley was dawdling, I could tell. Her suitcase finally got packed, but she left it in the guest room.

"We have to talk," she said.

My stomach clamped tight as a mousetrap.

"I've been talking to my brother and father, and somehow I get the feeling that what I have to do now is to start from the beginning. I need to go back to all the places I lived and talk to my family about it and come to terms with who I am. Who I *would* have been if Len and Ritchie hadn't stolen my life." Hayley sat on her bed and bounced up and down unconsciously, her boots tapping on the floor. "My brother is still friends with Stevie Wonder, and he's working with my old agent on a possible comeback. I'm not ready yet, but I have to take advantage of this moment, they tell me. They're even talking about a movie on my life!"

"A movie?"

"Yes! With possibly a book tie-in! Wouldn't *that* launch my career? I hate to think what some screenwriter could do with my story, but isn't the idea great?"

I allowed that it was. "What about Kitt?"

"What about her?"

"She's got a lot of ideas on how to help you get rolling. She said on the phone that a lot of people have been calling her, anxious for you to get back to L.A. Grace Slick wants to do some kind of sixties retro rock review with you. K.T. Oslin wrote you a song on stalking that she'll give to you outright. Janis Ian wants you as her opening act. Those are just a few of the people Kitt mentioned. I told you about them."

Hayley lay back on the bed and stretched as if she were afraid of fracturing her limbs if she pulled too hard. "I guess you did. I wasn't paying any attention. I'll have to talk to her too. I don't want to make the wrong decision. It's just that . . ." Even after her stretch she looked tense enough to shatter.

After an interminable length of time in which my stomach devoured itself, I had to prompt her. "It's just that what, Hayley?"

She rolled on her stomach and buried her face in her pillow.

"I need to be alone right now," she finally said. "I have this need to reconnect with my family, a need I didn't know was there. I lost so many years. I hurt so many people. I haven't a clue who the real me is. I walked down by the lake the other night and tried to sing some of my own songs, and I couldn't even imagine what I was feeling when I wrote them. I can't write a note, all I can do is perform everybody else's songs, and maybe that'll be enough. But I don't know if I'm good enough to even do that anymore."

I tried to sit down next to her on the bed to comfort her, to rub her back, but she waved me away.

"I'm going to call Patrick later on and ask if I can stay with him for a few weeks. For as long as it takes. He and his wife already asked me, and I said I didn't know. I can't go on in this daze. I have to start making some big decisions, and that's one I feel right about. Do you mind going back to L.A. alone, Laney?"

Of course I did. "If that's what you need, then that's what you have to do," I said. "I'm going to miss you every second you're gone, and I hope that eventually you'll come back. I'm going to miss you a lot." My voice choked.

She shot out of bed and put her arms around me and hugged me close. "I'm pretty sure I will be back, Laney. I love you. You've been the truest friend I've ever had. You and Kitt both. I want to come back to you. But I can't make that a promise right now. Do you understand?" Her pale eyes pleaded with me.

I nodded, unable to speak. I kissed her quickly on the lips and left.

The drive home was ungodly. I did it in three days, wired on coffee and memories. Radar whimpered a lot and kept asking for more stops.

When I got home Kitt put me to work on a dozen assignments to keep me busy. I had my overdue stitches to be removed. Mara, my AA sponsor, suggested I become a sponsor myself, and with my help two newcomers are busily thrashing through the twelve steps. Christmas is around the corner and my PR clients and the bar will need special promotions. This time of year is always hectic.

Meanwhile, I saw on "Entertainment Tonight" that Hayley had sold her story to one of the major studios for an astounding figure. They were talking about various people to play the roles, with Julia Roberts and Madonna being bandied about for the role of Hayley. They were looking for a young Jack Nicholson to play Ritchie. Kevin Bacon was a possible Len.

But the studio was really interested in only one person to play Hayley's love interest, the one who drove her back to Michigan to face down Ritchie and who rescued her from the burning barn. And silver-haired Richard Gere was reportedly very close to signing the contract.

A few of the publications of
THE NAIAD PRESS, INC.
P.O. Box 10543 • Tallahassee, Florida 32302
Phone (904) 539-5965
Toll-Free Order Number: 1-800-533-1973
Mail orders welcome. Please include 15% postage.

FLASHPOINT by Katherine V. Forrest. 256 pp. Lesbian
blockbuster! ISBN 1-56280-043-4 $22.95

CROSSWORDS by Penny Sumner. 256 pp. 2nd Victoria Cross
Mystery. ISBN 1-56280-064-7 9.95

SWEET CHERRY WINE by Carol Schmidt. 224 pp. A novel of
suspense. ISBN 1-56280-063-9 9.95

CERTAIN SMILES by Dorothy Tell. 160 pp. Erotic short stories
. ISBN 1-56280-066-3 9.95

EDITED OUT by Lisa Haddock. 224 pp. 1st Carmen Ramirez
Mystery. ISBN 1-56280-077-9 9.95

WEDNESDAY NIGHTS by Camarin Grae. 288 pp. Sexy
adventure. ISBN 1-56280-060-4 10.95

SMOKEY O by Celia Cohen. 176 pp. Relationships on the playing
field. ISBN 1-56280-057-4 9.95

KATHLEEN O'DONALD by Penny Hayes. 256 pp. Rose and
Kathleen find each other and employment in 1909 NYC.
ISBN 1-56280-070-1 9.95

STAYING HOME by Elisabeth Nonas. 256 pp. Molly and Alix
want a baby . . . or do they? ISBN 1-56280-076-0 10.95

TRUE LOVE by Jennifer Fulton. 240 pp. Six lesbians searching for
love in all the "right" places. ISBN 1-56280-035-3 9.95

GARDENIAS WHERE THERE ARE NONE by Molleen Zanger.
176 pp. Why is Melanie inextricably drawn to the old house?
ISBN 1-56280-056-6 9.95

MICHAELA by Sarah Aldridge. 256 pp. A "Sarah Aldridge"
romance. ISBN 1-56280-055-8 10.95

KEEPING SECRETS by Penny Mickelbury. 208 pp. A Gianna
Maglione Mystery. First in a series. ISBN 1-56280-052-3 9.95

THE ROMANTIC NAIAD edited by Katherine V. Forrest &
Barbara Grier. 336 pp. Love stories by Naiad Press authors.
ISBN 1-56280-054-X 14.95

UNDER MY SKIN by Jaye Maiman. 336 pp. A Robin Miller
mystery. 3rd in a series. ISBN 1-56280-049-3. 10.95

STAY TOONED by Rhonda Dicksion. 144 pp. Cartoons — 1st
collection since *Lesbian Survival Manual.* ISBN 1-56280-045-0 9.95

CAR POOL by Karin Kallmaker. 272pp. Lesbians on wheels
and then some! ISBN 1-56280-048-5 9.95

NOT TELLING MOTHER: STORIES FROM A LIFE by Diane
Salvatore. 176 pp. Her 3rd novel. ISBN 1-56280-044-2 9.95

GOBLIN MARKET by Lauren Wright Douglas. 240pp. A Caitlin
Reece Mystery. 5th in a series. ISBN 1-56280-047-7 9.95

LONG GOODBYES by Nikki Baker. 256 pp. A Virginia Kelly
mystery. 3rd in a series. ISBN 1-56280-042-6 9.95

FRIENDS AND LOVERS by Jackie Calhoun. 224 pp. Mid-western
Lesbian lives and loves. ISBN 1-56280-041-8 9.95

THE CAT CAME BACK by Hilary Mullins. 208 pp. Highly praised
Lesbian novel. ISBN 1-56280-040-X 9.95

BEHIND CLOSED DOORS by Robbi Sommers. 192 pp. Hot, erotic
short stories. ISBN 1-56280-039-6 9.95

CLAIRE OF THE MOON by Nicole Conn. 192 pp. See the movie —
read the book! ISBN 1-56280-038-8 10.95

SILENT HEART by Claire McNab. 192 pp. Exotic Lesbian
romance. ISBN 1-56280-036-1 9.95

HAPPY ENDINGS by Kate Brandt. 272 pp. Intimate conversations
with Lesbian authors. ISBN 1-56280-050-7 10.95

THE SPY IN QUESTION by Amanda Kyle Williams. 256 pp. 4th
Madison McGuire. ISBN 1-56280-037-X 9.95

SAVING GRACE by Jennifer Fulton. 240 pp. Adventure and
romantic entanglement. ISBN 1-56280-051-5 9.95

THE YEAR SEVEN by Molleen Zanger. 208 pp. Women surviving
in a new world. ISBN 1-56280-034-5 9.95

CURIOUS WINE by Katherine V. Forrest. 176 pp. Tenth
Anniversary Edition. The most popular contemporary Lesbian
love story. ISBN 1-56280-053-1 9.95

CHAUTAUQUA by Catherine Ennis. 192 pp. Exciting, romantic
adventure. ISBN 1-56280-032-9 9.95

A PROPER BURIAL by Pat Welch. 192 pp. A Helen Black
mystery. 3rd in a series. ISBN 1-56280-033-7 9.95

SILVERLAKE HEAT: A Novel of Suspense by Carol Schmidt.
240 pp. Rhonda is as hot as Laney's dreams. ISBN 1-56280-031-0 9.95

LOVE, ZENA BETH by Diane Salvatore. 224 pp. The most talked
about lesbian novel of the nineties! ISBN 1-56280-030-2 9.95

A DOORYARD FULL OF FLOWERS by Isabel Miller. 160 pp.
Stories incl. 2 sequels to *Patience and Sarah*. ISBN 1-56280-029-9   9.95

MURDER BY TRADITION by Katherine V. Forrest. 288 pp. A
Kate Delafield Mystery. 4th in a series. ISBN 1-56280-002-7   9.95

THE EROTIC NAIAD edited by Katherine V. Forrest & Barbara Grier.
224 pp. Love stories by Naiad Press authors. ISBN 1-56280-026-4   12.95

DEAD CERTAIN by Claire McNab. 224 pp. A Carol Ashton
mystery. 5th in a series. ISBN 1-56280-027-2   9.95

CRAZY FOR LOVING by Jaye Maiman. 320 pp. A Robin Miller
mystery. 2nd in a series. ISBN 1-56280-025-6   9.95

STONEHURST by Barbara Johnson. 176 pp. Passionate regency
romance. ISBN 1-56280-024-8   9.95

INTRODUCING AMANDA VALENTINE by Rose Beecham.
256 pp. An Amanda Valentine Mystery. First in a series.
ISBN 1-56280-021-3   9.95

UNCERTAIN COMPANIONS by Robbi Sommers. 204 pp.
Steamy, erotic novel. ISBN 1-56280-017-5   9.95

A TIGER'S HEART by Lauren W. Douglas. 240 pp. A Caitlin
Reece mystery. 4th in a series. ISBN 1-56280-018-3   9.95

PAPERBACK ROMANCE by Karin Kallmaker. 256 pp. A
delicious romance. ISBN 1-56280-019-1   9.95

MORTON RIVER VALLEY by Lee Lynch. 304 pp. Lee Lynch at
her best! ISBN 1-56280-016-7   9.95

THE LAVENDER HOUSE MURDER by Nikki Baker. 224 pp. A
Virginia Kelly Mystery. 2nd in a series. ISBN 1-56280-012-4   9.95

PASSION BAY by Jennifer Fulton. 224 pp. Passionate romance,
virgin beaches, tropical skies. ISBN 1-56280-028-0   9.95

STICKS AND STONES by Jackie Calhoun. 208 pp. Contemporary
lesbian lives and loves. ISBN 1-56280-020-5   9.95

DELIA IRONFOOT by Jeane Harris. 192 pp. Adventure for Delia
and Beth in the Utah mountains. ISBN 1-56280-014-0   9.95

UNDER THE SOUTHERN CROSS by Claire McNab. 192 pp.
Romantic nights Down Under. ISBN 1-56280-011-6   9.95

RIVERFINGER WOMEN by Elana Nachman/Dykewomon.
208 pp. Classic Lesbian/feminist novel. ISBN 1-56280-013-2   8.95

A CERTAIN DISCONTENT by Cleve Boutell. 240 pp. A unique
coterie of women. ISBN 1-56280-009-4   9.95

GRASSY FLATS by Penny Hayes. 256 pp. Lesbian romance in
the '30s. ISBN 1-56280-010-8   9.95

A SINGULAR SPY by Amanda K. Williams. 192 pp. 3rd Madison
McGuire. ISBN 1-56280-008-6   8.95

THE END OF APRIL by Penny Sumner. 240 pp. A Victoria Cross
Mystery. First in a series.   ISBN 1-56280-007-8   8.95

A FLIGHT OF ANGELS by Sarah Aldridge. 240 pp. Romance set at
the National Gallery of Art   ISBN 1-56280-001-9   9.95

HOUSTON TOWN by Deborah Powell. 208 pp. A Hollis Carpenter
mystery. Second in a series.   ISBN 1-56280-006-X   8.95

KISS AND TELL by Robbi Sommers. 192 pp. Scorching stories by
the author of *Pleasures*.   ISBN 1-56280-005-1   9.95

STILL WATERS by Pat Welch. 208 pp. A Helen Black mystery.
2nd in a series.   ISBN 0-941483-97-5   9.95

TO LOVE AGAIN by Evelyn Kennedy. 208 pp. Wildly
romantic love story.   ISBN 0-941483-85-1   9.95

IN THE GAME by Nikki Baker. 192 pp. A Virginia Kelly
mystery. First in a series.   ISBN 1-56280-004-3   9.95

AVALON by Mary Jane Jones. 256 pp. A Lesbian Arthurian
romance.   ISBN 0-941483-96-7   9.95

STRANDED by Camarin Grae. 320 pp. Entertaining, riveting
adventure.   ISBN 0-941483-99-1   9.95

THE DAUGHTERS OF ARTEMIS by Lauren Wright Douglas.
240 pp. A Caitlin Reece mystery. 3rd in a series.
                ISBN 0-941483-95-9   9.95

CLEARWATER by Catherine Ennis. 176 pp. Romantic secrets
of a small Louisiana town.   ISBN 0-941483-65-7   8.95

THE HALLELUJAH MURDERS by Dorothy Tell. 176 pp. A Poppy
Dillworth mystery. 2nd in a series.   ISBN 0-941483-88-6   8.95

ZETA BASE by Judith Alguire. 208 pp. Lesbian triangle
on a future Earth.   ISBN 0-941483-94-0   9.95

SECOND CHANCE by Jackie Calhoun. 256 pp. Contemporary
Lesbian lives and loves.   ISBN 0-941483-93-2   9.95

BENEDICTION by Diane Salvatore. 272 pp. Striking,
contemporary romantic novel.   ISBN 0-941483-90-8   9.95

CALLING RAIN by Karen Marie Christa Minns. 240 pp.
Spellbinding, erotic love story   ISBN 0-941483-87-8   9.95

BLACK IRIS by Jeane Harris. 192 pp. Caroline's hidden past . . .
                ISBN 0-941483-68-1   8.95

TOUCHWOOD by Karin Kallmaker. 240 pp. Loving, May/
December romance.   ISBN 0-941483-76-2   9.95

BAYOU CITY SECRETS by Deborah Powell. 224 pp. A Hollis
Carpenter mystery. First in a series.   ISBN 0-941483-91-6   9.95

COP OUT by Claire McNab. 208 pp. A Carol Ashton mystery.
4th in a series.   ISBN 0-941483-84-3   9.95

LODESTAR by Phyllis Horn. 224 pp. Romantic, fast-moving
adventure.   ISBN 0-941483-83-5   8.95

THE BEVERLY MALIBU by Katherine V. Forrest. 288 pp. A
Kate Delafield Mystery. 3rd in a series.   ISBN 0-941483-48-7   9.95

THAT OLD STUDEBAKER by Lee Lynch. 272 pp. Andy's affair
with Regina and her attachment to her beloved car.
                                          ISBN 0-941483-82-7   9.95

PASSION'S LEGACY by Lori Paige. 224 pp. Sarah is swept into
the arms of Augusta Pym in this delightful historical romance.
                                          ISBN 0-941483-81-9   8.95

THE PROVIDENCE FILE by Amanda Kyle Williams. 256 pp.
Second Madison McGuire   ISBN 0-941483-92-4   8.95

I LEFT MY HEART by Jaye Maiman. 320 pp. A Robin Miller
Mystery. First in a series.   ISBN 0-941483-72-X   9.95

THE PRICE OF SALT by Patricia Highsmith (writing as Claire
Morgan). 288 pp. Classic lesbian novel, first issued in 1952 . . .
acknowledged by its author under her own, very famous, name.
                                          ISBN 1-56280-003-5   9.95

SIDE BY SIDE by Isabel Miller. 256 pp. From beloved author of
Patience and Sarah.   ISBN 0-941483-77-0   9.95

STAYING POWER: LONG TERM LESBIAN COUPLES
by Susan E. Johnson. 352 pp. Joys of coupledom.
                                          ISBN 0-941-483-75-4   12.95

SLICK by Camarin Grae. 304 pp. Exotic, erotic adventure.
                                          ISBN 0-941483-74-6   9.95

NINTH LIFE by Lauren Wright Douglas. 256 pp. A Caitlin
Reece mystery. 2nd in a series.   ISBN 0-941483-50-9   8.95

PLAYERS by Robbi Sommers. 192 pp. Sizzling, erotic novel.
                                          ISBN 0-941483-73-8   9.95

MURDER AT RED ROOK RANCH by Dorothy Tell. 224 pp.
A Poppy Dillworth mystery. 1st in a series.   ISBN 0-941483-80-0   8.95

LESBIAN SURVIVAL MANUAL by Rhonda Dicksion.
112 pp. Cartoons!   ISBN 0-941483-71-1   8.95

A ROOM FULL OF WOMEN by Elisabeth Nonas. 256 pp.
Contemporary Lesbian lives.   ISBN 0-941483-69-X   9.95

PRIORITIES by Lynda Lyons 288 pp. Science fiction with
a twist.   ISBN 0-941483-66-5   8.95

THEME FOR DIVERSE INSTRUMENTS by Jane Rule. 208
pp. Powerful romantic lesbian stories.   ISBN 0-941483-63-0   8.95

LESBIAN QUERIES by Hertz & Ertman. 112 pp. The questions
you were too embarrassed to ask.   ISBN 0-941483-67-3   8.95

CLUB 12 by Amanda Kyle Williams. 288 pp. Espionage thriller
featuring a lesbian agent!   ISBN 0-941483-64-9   8.95

DEATH DOWN UNDER by Claire McNab. 240 pp. A Carol
Ashton mystery. 3rd in a series.   ISBN 0-941483-39-8   9.95

MONTANA FEATHERS by Penny Hayes. 256 pp. Vivian and
Elizabeth find love in frontier Montana.   ISBN 0-941483-61-4   8.95

CHESAPEAKE PROJECT by Phyllis Horn. 304 pp. Jessie &
Meredith in perilous adventure.   ISBN 0-941483-58-4   8.95

LIFESTYLES by Jackie Calhoun. 224 pp. Contemporary Lesbian
lives and loves.   ISBN 0-941483-57-6   9.95

VIRAGO by Karen Marie Christa Minns. 208 pp. Darsen has
chosen Ginny.   ISBN 0-941483-56-8   8.95

WILDERNESS TREK by Dorothy Tell. 192 pp. Six women on
vacation learning ''new'' skills.   ISBN 0-941483-60-6   8.95

MURDER BY THE BOOK by Pat Welch. 256 pp. A Helen
Black Mystery. First in a series.   ISBN 0-941483-59-2   9.95

LESBIANS IN GERMANY by Lillian Faderman & B. Eriksson.
128 pp. Fiction, poetry, essays.   ISBN 0-941483-62-2   8.95

THERE'S SOMETHING I'VE BEEN MEANING TO TELL
YOU Ed. by Loralee MacPike. 288 pp. Gay men and lesbians
coming out to their children.   ISBN 0-941483-44-4   9.95

LIFTING BELLY by Gertrude Stein. Ed. by Rebecca Mark. 104
pp. Erotic poetry.   ISBN 0-941483-51-7   8.95

ROSE PENSKI by Roz Perry. 192 pp. Adult lovers in a long-term
relationship.   ISBN 0-941483-37-1   8.95

AFTER THE FIRE by Jane Rule. 256 pp. Warm, human novel
by this incomparable author.   ISBN 0-941483-45-2   8.95

SUE SLATE, PRIVATE EYE by Lee Lynch. 176 pp. The gay
folk of Peacock Alley are *all cats.*   ISBN 0-941483-52-5   8.95

CHRIS by Randy Salem. 224 pp. Golden oldie. Handsome Chris
and her adventures.   ISBN 0-941483-42-8   8.95

THREE WOMEN by March Hastings. 232 pp. Golden oldie. A
triangle among wealthy sophisticates.   ISBN 0-941483-43-6   8.95

RICE AND BEANS by Valeria Taylor. 232 pp. Love and
romance on poverty row.   ISBN 0-941483-41-X   8.95

PLEASURES by Robbi Sommers. 204 pp. Unprecedented
eroticism.   ISBN 0-941483-49-5   8.95

EDGEWISE by Camarin Grae. 372 pp. Spellbinding
adventure.   ISBN 0-941483-19-3   9.95

FATAL REUNION by Claire McNab. 224 pp. A Carol Ashton
mystery. 2nd in a series.   ISBN 0-941483-40-1   8.95

KEEP TO ME STRANGER by Sarah Aldridge. 372 pp. Romance
set in a department store dynasty.   ISBN 0-941483-38-X   9.95

IN THE BLOOD by Lauren Wright Douglas. 252 pp. Lesbian
science fiction adventure fantasy   ISBN 0-941483-22-3   8.95

THE BEE'S KISS by Shirley Verel. 216 pp. Delicate, delicious
romance.   ISBN 0-941483-36-3   8.95

RAGING MOTHER MOUNTAIN by Pat Emmerson. 264 pp.
Furosa Firechild's adventures in Wonderland.   ISBN 0-941483-35-5   8.95

IN EVERY PORT by Karin Kallmaker. 228 pp. Jessica's sexy,
adventuresome travels.   ISBN 0-941483-37-7   9.95

OF LOVE AND GLORY by Evelyn Kennedy. 192 pp. Exciting
WWII romance.   ISBN 0-941483-32-0   8.95

CLICKING STONES by Nancy Tyler Glenn. 288 pp. Love
transcending time.   ISBN 0-941483-31-2   9.95

SURVIVING SISTERS by Gail Pass. 252 pp. Powerful love
story.   ISBN 0-941483-16-9   8.95

SOUTH OF THE LINE by Catherine Ennis. 216 pp. Civil War
adventure.   ISBN 0-941483-29-0   8.95

WOMAN PLUS WOMAN by Dolores Klaich. 300 pp. Supurb
Lesbian overview.   ISBN 0-941483-28-2   9.95

HEAVY GILT by Delores Klaich. 192 pp. Lesbian detective/
disappearing homophobes/upper class gay society.
                                          ISBN 0-941483-25-8   8.95

THE FINER GRAIN by Denise Ohio. 216 pp. Brilliant young
college lesbian novel.   ISBN 0-941483-11-8   8.95

HIGH CONTRAST by Jessie Lattimore. 264 pp. Women of the
Crystal Palace.   ISBN 0-941483-17-7   8.95

OCTOBER OBSESSION by Meredith More. Josie's rich, secret
Lesbian life.   ISBN 0-941483-18-5   8.95

BEFORE STONEWALL: THE MAKING OF A GAY AND
LESBIAN COMMUNITY by Andrea Weiss & Greta Schiller.
96 pp., 25 illus.   ISBN 0-941483-20-7   7.95

WE WALK THE BACK OF THE TIGER by Patricia A. Murphy.
192 pp. Romantic Lesbian novel/beginning women's movement.
                                          ISBN 0-941483-13-4   8.95

SUNDAY'S CHILD by Joyce Bright. 216 pp. Lesbian athletics, at
last the novel about sports.   ISBN 0-941483-12-6   8.95

These are just a few of the many Naiad Press titles — we are the oldest and
largest lesbian/feminist publishing company in the world. Please request a
complete catalog. We offer personal service; we encourage and welcome direct
mail orders from individuals who have limited access to bookstores carrying
our publications.